Enjoy , thank

# The Turnings of the Years

Daisy Hufferdine.

# The Turnings of the Years
## A collection of short stories
by
## Llandovery Writers' Group and Friends.

### Contributors:

Helen Adam
Peter Barker
Phil Carradice
Joy Daniels
Sara Fox
Kate Glanville
Julian Gray
Daisy Hufferdine
Jacquie Hyde
Steve Kill
Will Macmillan-Jones
Ciaran O Connell
Colin R. Parsons
Tom Phelps
Hazel Redgrave
Maya Sales-Hyde
Sally Spedding
Stella Starnes
John Thompson
David Thorpe
Mary Thurgate
Graham Watkins

Publisher Garnlwyd Publishing
2018

photograph by Elodie Rose Hamaide. Cover design by cyberium.co.uk

ISBN  978-0-244-71757-5

Garnlwyd Publishing
Garnlwyd, Gwynfe,
Llangadog, Carmarthenshire. SA19 9PU

graham@garnlwyd.co.uk

# Dedication

To the people who freely give their time and experience
helping others.
All profit generated by the sales of this book will be donated to
support Llandovery Youth and Community Centre.

# Contents

## Sacred Vows
## By Ciaran O Connell

It was New Year's Day. Father Patrick O'Toole woke with a mild hangover. Last night had been fun. Their housekeeper had excelled herself and the three men had sat down to a delicious roast dinner with perhaps too many glasses of red wine.

Once they had scraped the last of the Christmas pudding, drenched in double cream and well soaked in brandy, they sat back and watched indulgently as Mrs Moore cleared the table. O'Toole, a man more used to complaining about his lot, did admit to himself that the life of a parish curate living in a presbytery across the road from his church wasn't all bad.

Stretching out the last dregs of the wine the two curates gossiped together about the events of the Christmas week, who had the most difficult of masses, who had been stuck with the most boring parishioners at the old people's Boxing Day lunch, and finally, which was the best Christmas film on the television. Father O'Brien, the Parish Priest, did not join in their chatter. Instead he sat and watched silently as the older curate tried to solidify his place as number two in the clerical pecking order. O'Toole had come to the parish as a curate twenty-two years earlier. He was still a curate. The other chap, in his late twenties, had come straight from the seminary less than a year ago. When O'Brien saw that their glasses were at last empty, he slapped one hand down on the table.

'Fathers, let me offer you both a proper drink.' He turned in his chair, bent down and unlocked a small oak cupboard behind him.

When he turned back he reverently placed a dark green bottle in the middle of the table. O'Toole 's eyes lit up. It was Ardbeg - one of Islay's greatest malt whiskies.

'A Christmas gift from one of the parishioners,' O'Brien announced with a rare smile. 'I thought we could see in the New Year with a wee drop or two. Father O'Toole, ask Mrs Moore for some suitable glasses please.'

He was happy to obey and soon returned with three Waterford crystal glasses and a small jug of water.

Nearing midnight they took their drinks out into the garden. From the patio they had a clear view of fireworks going off all around the parish.

It was the morning of the first day of the New Year. The sun, spilling through the bedroom curtains, brought a smile to his face. He lay back in his bed, savouring the unusually bright January weather and trying to ignore his throbbing head. 'Not a bad price to pay for those few glasses of heaven.' he told himself.

It was then that he remembered what day of the week it was – Saturday. It was bloody Saturday. New Year's Day or not, it was still O'Toole's turn to spend his morning listening to the sins of the faithful.

'God, how I hate Confession,' he said. 'It's so boring.'

He looked at his clock – coming up to eight. Enough time for breakfast.

Father O'Toole had been hearing confessions every Saturday since he first arrived in the parish. In that time he had never once heard anything even mildly juicy or interesting: Lying to a husband, a wife, a mother or father, stealing from the company stationery cupboard, a quick fumble with somebody's wife or girlfriend at an office party, swearing, spreading malicious gossip. The litany of sins, all of them little sins, boring little sins were repeated week after week, and year after year. A couple of times he would get to hear tales of husbands or wives deceiving one another. He had to admit that the adulteries did hold a bit of a thrill for him. He often had to pull himself back from asking for a little more detail than was necessary.

It was nine thirty when he entered the church. The kneeling queue outside the confessional already filled two pews. He stepped into his box, drew across the thick velvet curtain and switched on the red light that told the world Father Patrick O'Toole was ready for duty. Three hours later he was still sitting there. He had taken a quick break around eleven for a pee and a quick fag. He had managed to stretch that to fifteen minutes without causing too much upset to the waiting penitents. But he was bored. He was bored when he arrived and he was still bored. He wondered if the queue outside was getting any shorter.

He had just seen off a young boy whose confessional highlight had been stealing a couple of pounds from his mother's purse. O'Toole delivered absolution along with his standard kid's penance, one decade of the rosary and a promise not to do it again. He started thinking about lunch. Mrs Moore was the best cook he had ever had the good fortune to be fed by. It was to be Spaghetti Carbonara today. His favourite.

As the boy opened the door to leave, a shaft of light allowed him to see the time on his watch - a quarter to one. She always dished up at one on the dot. He knew that if you weren't there on time, your share would soon disappear.

'I'm calling it a day after this one,' he told himself. The penitent's door open. A few creaks, coupled with a strong smell of stale tobacco mixed up with cheap perfume, and then more creaking as the person knelt down facing the grill. Over the years he had amused himself by guessing the weight of the penitent based on the level of creaking produced.

"A bit on the weighty side I would say,' he told himself. 'At least it's not another pilfering child.'

He drew open the screen and leaned back in his chair. As always he had to resist taking a quick glance through the grill. He knew it was wrong of him. But the urge never went away.

'Bless me father for I have sinned…' The words stumbled out slowly in a rasping voice. She was a smoker all right.

'How long has it been since your last confession?'

'I don't know father. I'm not sure.'

'A week, a month, a rough idea will do.'

'Probably more like nine or ten years.'

He groaned inwardly. This was going to be a long one. He imagined the conversation back at the presbytery lunch table. 'He's probably been held up.' Father O'Brien would be the first to speak. No point in wasting his share.' The young curate would be nodding vigorously in agreement. 'He'll probably get something later.'

Ten years,' he wailed silently. 'This is going to take forever.'

'So, tell me your sins my child.'

The woman was in no hurry. There was silence. He clasped his hands together. After a few more moments he gave out a little cough.

'Well, let me think Father. It's been such a long time. I'm not sure I'll be able to remember all of them but I'll have a go. '

What followed was a slowly delivered list of lies, petty stealing, excessive drinking, and a couple of sexual exploits that did nothing to raise his interest. All delivered in halting phrases, short bursts of words with long pauses in between. He offered no comments, just kept nudging her on with the occasional 'and what else?' or 'yes my child' thrown in to keep her moving forward.

Finally she reached a pause that went on longer than the any of earlier ones.

'Is that the lot then?' He tried to keep the sense of urgency out of his voice. The curtain that hid him from the outside world let in next to no light. Certainly not enough for him to have another look at the dial on his watch. Now if she would just open her door and go….

'Well Father… there is one more thing. To be honest It's actually the reason I came to see you.'

'Now is time to make your peace with Our Lord my child.' He pursed his lips and raised his eyes to heaven. 'What is it?'

'I don't know how to tell you father.'

O'Toole wanted desperately to know the time. He took a deep breath. He gritted his teeth. He forced himself into a smile and turned to address the grill.

'Just tell it to God my child.' All concern about keeping the irritation from his voice now forgotten. He could hear her painful breathing on the other side of the grill. There was another long pause.

He waited, and waited. He didn't notice that his left foot was tapping repeatedly against the oak-panelled floor. When she did speak, her voice was nearer to a whisper.

'It's murder Father.'

The priest sat upright. Did he hear that right? 'What did you say? Did you say 'murder'?'

'Yes Father. That's right. Murder. That's a mortal sin, isn't it?'

'Yes, of course it's a mortal sin.' He leaned forward now. This was exciting. He had never had a murder before. 'What's this about? Are you telling me you have committed a murder?'

'Yes and no Father.'

'Yes and no! What do you mean 'yes and no'?' The woman was making no sense. 'Either you have killed somebody or you haven't. Which is it woman?'

'Well...' Another pause. 'Can I confess to murder now Father. Even though I haven't done it yet?'

Father O'Toole was in unknown territory now. Heaven knows what sort of a person he was dealing with. Was the woman unstable? Was she going to do something dreadful? In the dark of the cubicle the priest shook his head silently. Get a grip, he told himself, calm down.

'Good God woman. What are you telling me? No you can't! Of course you can't!' He wasn't quite shouting but if there were anybody left outside the cubicle they would have heard his anger.

'Sorry Father, I'm sorry. It's my Billy.' The words spilled out fast now, tumbling over each other as if a dam had burst. 'The thing is you see, I've had enough. If I don't do him in I'll end up topping myself. And that's a sin too Father isn't it.'

'No it's not. Suicide is not classified as a sin anymore.' The priest tried hard to keep the irritation out of his voice. This woman was definitely trouble. He had to remind himself that she was also clearly in trouble.

'Who is this Billy that you say you want to kill?'

'He's my husband, Father.'

'Let me get this clear. Are you telling me that you plan to kill your husband? And you want me, I mean God, to forgive you for it even before you have done it?

'That's about the size of it Father.'

'I'm very sorry but that's not possible. I can't give you forgiveness for something you haven't done.'

He waited for her to say more. But the black space beyond the grill stayed silent. Save for the struggling breath. 'I strongly urge you to think again. You will be caught and will probably spend the rest of your days in prison. Why do you want to kill this poor man?'

'Think of your children. Do you have any children by the way?'

'I do, Father. Two girls. Anne will be eighteen in March. God knows where she is now. She's been gone since her sixteenth birthday. She calls me on the phone every few months. But she never tells me where she is.

'And that's why I have to do it soon. Evie will be ten next week. He's already started sniffing around. He won't leave her alone. I'm not having it father. He's not going to do her like he did with poor Anne. Not this time.

'I've thought it all out. I'm going to make it look like an accident. I'm pretty sure I won't be caught. Then me and Evie will be okay. Anne might even come back when she hears.'

Father O'Toole struggled, but could think of nothing to say. Silence stole into the confessional. Who is this woman, he thought. I'm sure I recognise the voice.

'Anyway Father, you've given me the answer. Not what I wanted to hear, but there you go. I suppose I'll have to come back next week and tell it to you all over again. Don't worry. I won't be wasting your time. I'll have it done by then.'

There was a rustle, the door opened, and she was gone. She hadn't even waited for absolution. O'Toole pulled the curtain back a little. The place was empty except for a short, overweight woman walking slowly toward the back of the church. As she turned to open the doors he caught a quick look at her face. He recognised her. He couldn't quite recall the name though he remembered the family. They lived somewhere on that big estate on the way into the town centre.

He sat back in his cubicle and closed his eyes. In all his years in the confessional this was a first for him. It was now half one. He switched off his red light, stepped out of his box and left the church.

The road was busy. Cars speeding past in both directions. There was the presbytery directly across on the other side. He stood looking at the solid Georgian house. The minutes ticked by and still he stood there. Every now and then some of the cars would stop to let him cross. But he waved them on. He looked down the hill towards the town. He could see the tops of the estate tower blocks.

On the other side of the main road, though he couldn't see it from where he stood, sat the police station. He looked back at the house. He could see Father O'Brien now. He was standing in the window of the lounge, looking out at him. He would know the right thing to do. The old priest waved at him. O'Toole waved back, turned left and started walking.

# The Reckoning
## By Graham Watkins

'Due to me this day £4. 7s and...'

Ink falls from the nib onto the page. It runs, like a tiny black stream, across the words. I return the pen to the inkwell and blot the mess. The kitchen door opens. Water drips across the tiles. A bucket scrapes the floor. Jane is humming as she places it by the fire. She always hums when she works; a busy tune - a rhythm to pace herself. She removes her coat and puts on a clean pinny, tying it at the front. I watch her press a loaf tight against chest, butter it and cut a wafer thin slice. My mother used to slice bread the same way. Plum jam is in the china bowl she fetches from the cupboard. I close my diary.

It's been a long year. Last winter was so cold the river turned to ice. So cold our sow froze in her pen. I found her stiff and lifeless. Snow blocked the lane until March.

Jane places a cup and saucer on the table. Both are chipped and cracked. Her best cups, for admiring, are on the dresser. She lifts a pot from the hearth and pours. I tip the steaming tea into my saucer and blow to cool the scalding brew. I sip from the saucer, still too hot. I blow again.

The breakfast things are cleared away. Jane takes the bucket and fills the kettle hanging in the chimney. She adds twigs to the red embers. They burst into life, spitting and crackling. Flames dance across the grate. I watch her carve a wedge from the flitch of bacon curing above the hearth. She dices the meat and adds it to the stew-pot warming beside the oven. By tonight the meat will be tender.

Spring came late and I was greatly relieved by its arrival. The snow gone, the roads passable and, at last, I had a chance to work, to earn some money. Mr. Davis' barn needed a new roof. He offered me three pounds to do the work. I borrowed his cart and old nag to fetch timber from the railway station. Driving down into the valley I stopped in the river to let the horse drink, to soak the wheels and tighten the rims. The station master, in his crisp uniform, stood and watched me with suspicion as I loaded the stout oak planks. The rough sawn timber was heavy, like iron. We left the station at a slow walk. Climbing from the valley the horse strained in its traces then stumbled, regained its footing and stopped. I used the whip but the animal was finished and refused to go a step further. Three days it took me to haul the timber to the farm.

Mr. Davis is a careful man, some say mean.

'You abused my horse.' He spat on the ground. 'And damaged my cart.'

Two weeks of sweat and all he would pay was one pound eight shillings; scant reward for my labour. But, it was money and I was sore in need of it.

The day he paid me I bought Jane a fine red shawl for two shillings and four pence. She was pleased with her present but refused to wear it. Instead, she carefully folded it in brown paper. 'It's too new for every day,' she said and packed it in the drawer where she kept her special things.

My diary is open again. I flick back to July, a sad time for us all. We buried our dear boy Jacob that month. Scarlet fever took him from us three days before his fourth birthday. I shudder to remember his screams as the doctor shaved his head and scraped pustules from his scalp. Poor Jacob struggled, as I held him tight, writhing to escape the leeches clinging to his temple.

'They will remove the poison from his blood,' explained the doctor, but the leeches didn't remove the poison. He was a brave little boy til the end. I used some of Mr. Davis' oak, off cuts I'd taken, to make his tiny coffin. Jane lined it with a grey blanket to keep his little body warm in the ground.

The snow has started again. Wind is blowing flakes through a crack in the kitchen door. Jane points to the fire. I take my coat from behind the door and fetch wood from the shed. The yard is covered in brown slush.

'Will next year be the same?' I wonder as I stack logs by the fire.

A whimper from the crib. Alice cries. Jane picks her up and holds her to her breast. Alice sucks greedily.

We christened Alice last August one week after we laid Jacob to rest. It was a hot day. Villagers filled the church that Sunday and welcomed Alice into the world but I cried as we passed the little pile of earth covering where Jacob lay.

Jane has changed the baby and she sleeps. There's a knock at the door, loud and insistent. I know who it is; the rent collector, Mr. Williams. The door opens. Uninvited, Mr. Williams steps into the kitchen chilling the room with cold air. Dirty snow falls from his boots.

'Do you have it?' he demands.

I take the money tin from the dresser, count out one pound ten shillings and hand it to him.

'It's not enough. You're six weeks behind. I require another thirty shillings or the bailiffs will be calling,' he growls.

'Sit down Mr. Williams,' says Jane. 'The kettle is boiling. I'll make some tea.'

Mr. Williams removes his hat and sits awkwardly at the table. I shut the diary and move it away from him. Williams is a brute of a man, a bully, but Jane has his measure. She smiles at him as she pours the tea then busies herself around the kitchen. Has he noticed her face is turned away?

He drinks, tells us he's a reasonable man, that he'll give us an extra week to find the money we owe. He smiles at Jane, lecherous swine, and goes on his way, to the next cottage where the scene will likely be repeated. Jane isn't smiling, now he's gone. I make a note of how much we've paid Mr. Williams in my diary.

Frost and foggy mornings warned the year was turning. It was September. The days grew shorter, the nights colder. I worked until dusk each day to lay Mr. Hughes' hedges. He owed me £2. 4shillings and promised to pay before Michelmas but the 29th September passed and he didn't honour the debt. I killed our weaner on the 30th. Jane helped gut the pig and salt the meat. We would not starve this winter. Mrs Jones traded us a sack of flour for a bowl of brawn Jane made from the pig's head. Jane interrupts my thoughts. 'You must find the money for the rent man.'

I promise I'll see farmer Hughes and get what he owes me. It's a faint hope but I can't tell Jane that he has no money for fear of worrying her. The mixing bowl comes out. She removes the cloth covering the risen dough, kneads it once more and sets it on a baking tray to rise again. Satisfied it's ready, she pushes it into the hot oven. The door shuts and latches with a metallic click. As I write my journal, the kitchen fills with the smell of baking bread; warm, comforting, safe. How lucky we are, how lucky I am. God has blessed us this last year but he has also tested us. Did he take little Jacob because I doubted him? I shudder at the idea, the cruelty of such a God.

'You missed two Sundays,' said the vicar after Jacob's funeral. 'God is watching us all. He knows everything.' The vicar is a pompous, pious man. I've never liked him.

October brought great excitement to the village. The Queen was coming. Our Queen, Empress of three quarters of the world would soon be here. We dressed in our Sunday clothes and walked three miles, through the mud, to the railway station. A hawker was selling paper flags for two pence each. We stood on the platform and waited. Jane looked grand in her fine new shawl, her face as rosy as the red wool. She wrapped the shawl around Alice to keep out the cold. Someone started to sing, 'Rule Britannia, Britannia rules the...' Others joined in. 'Britains never, never, never will be slaves...' We were excited and proud. Victoria, our Queen was coming.

A steam whistle echoed along the valley; shrill, discordant.

'The Queen. A train. The Queen's coming,' yelled a youth.

'God save the Queen,' chorused the crowd as the train approached.

The engine passed with a roar, hissing steam, belching soot and black smoke. We strained to glimpse the royal passenger in the carriages as they rattled past. The windows were misted, blinds drawn.

Jane screamed and clutched at her face.

'It's burning,' she shrieked. Something was in her eye, a hot cinder blown from the engine. And then, the train was gone. Her right eye was red and weeping. Walking home, we stopped at the stream and bathed it.

'Did you see her, the Queen?' asked Jane.

That terrible October day when Jane lost her eye is seared in my memory.

I open the diary at today's date, 31st December 1866, dip my pen in the inkwell and complete my annual reckoning.

'Due to me this day          £4. 7s   6d.

I owe          £2. 18s 11d.

Balance in my favour          £1. 8s   7d.

May God watch over us and grant us a good life in the coming year.'


The ink dries slowly on the page. Another year is done.

# First Christmas In Africa
By Hazel Redgrave

Liverpool, 1948. My father had accepted employment in what was then Tanganyika, now Tanzania. It had seemed exciting after the dreariness of the war years, but it meant that he had to travel by flying boat, which took a week in those days, and he had to go alone because the men were to live in tents for that first year and conditions were very Spartan. However during that time family housing was built so that wives and children could follow later. My father said his goodbyes to my mother, sister and I, hoisted his kit bag onto his shoulders and was gone. We were not to see him for a year.

The house in Liverpool was sold; my mother, my sister Rose and I travelled by train to London to join the ship Llangibby Castle – one of the many Union Castle liners which travelled around Africa, either via the Suez Canal which took four weeks, or via the Cape which took six. I was eight years of age, Rose was three. The ship broke down at Aden and we were stuck there for two weeks, waiting for a spare part to be sent from the UK. The heat was intense and very uncomfortable and no breeze of any kind came through the portholes. Pieces of cardboard would be wedged in a semi-circle within the open porthole, but this only created a breeze if the ship was moving. The monotony was relieved by local vendors who would ply their trade from little boats around the ship, sending up goods for us to see via ropes and baskets. Small boys would dive for coins tossed into the sea by passengers.

In due course we arrived at our destination, Dar-es-Salaam (Haven of Peace), on the east coast of Tanganyika. It is a beautiful but shallow harbour, and the ship docked some way from the shore. We waited and waited for my father to come for us via a small launch - but – no Dad! Eventually we got into a launch ourselves and chug-chugged to shore. As we did so, another launch passed us and I heard my mother shout out 'there's my Harry!' and she began     waving energetically. Our launch was heading for the jetty but Dad was going the opposite way towards the ship and, although it seemed ages, we eventually got together about twenty minutes later. There was much hugging and kissing, and once through the formality of Customs we made for the Metropole Hotel. Mother looked at the gaping lift shaft in the hotel – there were no gates, just a long drop down. 'We're not staying here,' she said firmly, and we decamped for the Splendid Hotel instead.

After a few days we took a long train journey, a day and half a night, to a place called Kongwa, the seat of the British Government's ill-thought-out 'Groundnut Scheme' where my father worked, and eventually we settled down in the newly-built house, and got used to a very different life to that of the privations and bomb damage of Liverpool. Sweets were still on the ration in the UK at that time and restrictions were not lifted until 1953. There were strange things to get used to, for example our hot water supply was a 44-gallon oil drum, laid on its side over brick supports and a fire lit beneath it. It was kept alight at all times and a metal pipe snaked across the garden from it, and into the taps inside the house. Clothes were ironed with a charcoal iron. Glowing lumps of charcoal were put inside the hollow iron to heat it, and from time to time it would be swung to and fro, to increase the air flow and dislodge some of the ashes. Most of our clothes bore evidence of the damage caused by hot sparks which frequently landed on them during this process. There were many things which we had to become accustomed to, including having to boil all of our drinking water, then filter it in large ceramic filters.

To celebrate our first Christmas in Africa we cut down a large thorn bush which acted as a Christmas tree, and my sister and I decorated it as best we could. We had both just recovered from chicken pox – me for the second time – and it was good to have something to look forward to. My mother made a superb Christmas cake, something she was very good at, and she managed to make marzipan from whole almonds by crushing them with a rolling pin. Her icing had to be seen to be believed; she was very professional and iced in the old-fashioned way, trailing lines of icing over shapes in a  trellis pattern and letting them dry, then transferring these raised domes to the cake and icing little flowers around each one. By the time she had finished pushing the royal icing through the little syringe, the palm of her right hand was red and very sore indeed – it took a lot of effort and a great deal of patience.

Christmas Eve arrived and there was much happy anticipation as we got ready for bed, giggling and not at all tired, wondering what we would get in the way of presents, knowing that they would be better than the rather meagre gifts we had received in wartime Liverpool. At about 2am I woke my sister and we looked at the pillow cases which had been stacked at the ends of our beds, trying to feel what might be within. In the end it was easier to creep into the lounge with the sacks, tip-toeing quietly and closing the door behind us. We were lucky - it was the rainy season and the tropical rain was thundering noisily on the corrugated iron roof, drowning out any noise we might be making. We waited for a moment – no sound from the parents' room – so we bravely turned on the light and began to dig into the pillow cases in earnest. I had a huge book – 'Orlando, the Marmalade Cat' (I have it still) and lots of smaller gifts. But the presents which made us gasp the most were two seaside buckets on the sides of which were pictures of happy children building sandcastles on the beach. The buckets had lids which, when lifted, revealed the treasure within – Blue Bird Toffees – lots and lots of toffees! We had never seen so many sweets and I am afraid that we rather gorged ourselves.

It was about this time that we realised we were not alone. Millions and millions of flying ants were swirling around the room, coming in their masses under the gap in the outside door, attracted by the light. Once they had landed they shed their wings and could not take off again, so they crawled everywhere - up our pyjama legs and over our arms, into our hair - and we had to shake them off, swatting this way and that trying to get rid of them noiselessly so as not to awaken our parents. We were used to creepy-crawlies in East Africa, but on this scale it was overwhelming. In the end it got so bad we abandoned our Christmas presents, turned off the light and crept back into our bedroom - having the presence of mind to take our Blue Bird treasure with us! Sometime later our cook prepared some ants in the kitchen for us to try, but father was the only one who was brave enough to eat any. He declared he found them 'interesting', but the ants were extremely popular with the indigenous people. If they longed for some out of season they would cover an anthill with cloths and gently drum on the ground for a while. Believing it to be raining the ants would emerge, only to be captured for lunch!

We got used to many things during our years in East Africa – snakes, scorpions, safari ants, white ants which tried to eat us out of house and home, hyenas, little velvety-red rain beetles – all manner of unusual creatures. But the experience which stands out in my mind, even now, was that first Christmas in East Africa at the turning of the year from 1949 to 1950, nearly seventy years ago.

# That Summer

By Sara Fox

'Wanna come down the park?' Manda hung above me in the ash tree, a dark shape blotting out the sun. I was lying on a towel on the hot felt roof of the shed, with a book and a half full glass of warm barley water that had left a bitter clogged feeling in the back of my mouth.

'Alright.' I climbed onto the tree and jumped down the last few feet. The holidays had been going on for a hundred years and I was bored. Bored with being at home, with my mother, and even with the heat. The novelty of sun all day and every day was shortening the tempers of children and adults. A low rumble of thunder was present in most houses in the avenue and still the sky remained an unremitting blue.

We went through the dark kitchen and hallway, into the glare of the street, past the uniform rows of French marigolds and lobelias, an orange and blue militia that patrolled the front paths. The more experimental gardens had dwarf weeping willows or contorted cherries that dominated the tiny front lawns. We skulked past Mrs Smith's garden with its laburnum, laden with splitting pods of poisonous black seeds that she policed in a darting manner from behind her hedge.

We had forgotten what rain was and lived in swimming costumes and flip flops, attracting wasps with the juice that ran down our chins from frozen Jubblys; those inaccessible tetrahedrons from the sweet shop on the Radleys. Today we were barefoot, stubbing toes on the hot pavement. Crossing roads, coating the soles of our feet with sticky black tar that leaked seismically from cracks in the tarmac. Pungent gusts from creosoted telegraph poles cleared our nostrils and dusty cats and dogs lay at full stretch in narrow panels of shade between the houses. We passed the gully-ways where fathers tinkered in their garages with obscure metallic clankings.

Single-file we entered the passageway between the football pitches and the park proper. I dragged my fingers along the dusty chain link fence. In front of me Manda methodically tore strips of peeling skin from her shoulder, the result of a spectacular sunburn acquired a week earlier at Pontins.

The car factory kids all went on holiday in the last week of term. This was another keenly felt injustice. I had the regulation six weeks only.

Turning left, we followed the path to the brook lined with scrubby trees. Six months older than me, Manda had just scaled the forbidding heights of a year at the Comp. In her position as guru to me the uninitiated, she felt it incumbent upon her to delineate all of its horrors in full Panavision. 'Guess what? In Sex Education we draw diagrams of willies. They are called penises. Men put them up ya, then you 'av a babby!'

'That's really horrible.' I was shocked to the core but determined not to show it. How terrible life was turning out after all. Manda's bald statement was indisputably true and made the vague utterances by my mother regarding the origin of babies seem like stupid lies. Moving to The Comp now felt like a prison sentence with a 'here are the facts' re-education programme.

We sat on the bridge by the swings, our legs burning on the hot concrete. Leaning our arms on the metal bars we looked down at the broken bricks and glass glinting in the honey coloured water of the brook. Manda licked the salty moisture on her top lip thoughtfully. We had finished our sweets, a sherbet dibdab for Manda and a quarter of mixed chews. I, much to the disgust of the man in the shop, had asked for 150 mini teddy babies at 3 for 1p. Pocket money expended in half an hour, we allowed our stomachs to distend queasily.

The sun had bleached everything yellow, the grass, old chip papers, our hair. Manda's blonde shock was now strawy in texture and stood out from her skull at odd angles. My dull, brown hair had been transformed. I now had a golden streak down one side of my parting. I was well aware of this lustrous, unlooked-for beauty and ran my fingers along it endlessly, pulling it towards my nose and mouth to catch sight of the miracle from crossed eyes.

Irritated, Manda cast a cold eye upon me. Grabbing my arm, she proceeded to administer a particularly vicious Chinese burn. Small tortures were her stock in trade. Resentfully pushing her brother's pram up to the shops, she would stop to pinch him if he cried. This was counter-productive and a long drawn out wailing always ensued. He was an unattractive, featureless baby, but nevertheless he did not deserve Manda as a big sister.

I wrenched my arm free. 'Geroff you Cow!' Manda released her grip and smiled. I never paid her back for anything really, her power always remained unchallenged. She began a new attack. 'Eh, Elvis is dead, did you 'ear?' Pinpricks of painful liquid gathered behind my eyes. 'Stop lying!' I shouted, but knew it was true by the flash of triumph in Manda's pale, gobstopper orbs.

The world wobbled on its axis for a few moments then I pulled myself up and started walking purposefully away from the bridge and the swings, following the sluggish brook where the park narrowed, pinched by the garages behind the houses on one side and the football fields on the other. I stumbled a couple of times, pebble-eyed, large teardrops threatening to fall. Manda was running along the path behind me. *I won't cry, wouldn't give her the satisfaction.* I heard her call but stubbornly carried on, her shouts faded, and I realised she had given up and was probably sauntering back to the avenue in search of another victim.

After a few minutes I trailed after her, tracking her covertly. Near her back fence I could hear joyful shouts and splashing water. They had the hosepipe out. I gingerly clambered up a solidified hillock of garden waste, contorting myself to avoid the menacingly tall and venomous nettles. Grasping the top of the fence I pulled myself up until my legs were hanging. Manda's cousins from Halesowen were running amuck in her garden. I thought about calling out to them but knew I would not be welcome when relatives were there. Manda's mum had a short fuse, especially where too many children were concerned. They interfered with her cleaning and watching International Athletics with the curtains drawn. I could see the pop man had been; four glasses of Dandelion and Burdock were balanced on the crazy paving. Sensible, dull Ribena waited at home for me.

Manda had her cousins busily employed plucking the petals from her mother's bed of floribunda roses that rioted in a profusion of

24

Technicolor red, orange and yellow. They were going to make perfume. We had made some disappointing attempts in that dark art at my house. My mother's veranda was now full of pots of stinking brown and viscous liquid.

An angular shadow appeared at the kitchen window and next thing Manda's mother shot out onto the patio. I felt the air crackle with static. Manda was beckoned indoors. I heard her mother's high-pitched complaint and Manda's whining response followed by a slap like a starter pistol, then sudden silence.

A minute or two passed, my arms were really starting to ache now, and my hands were marsupial claws welded by rigor mortis to the top of the fence. Manda reappeared in the garden head down, with the livid mark of her mother's hand on her cheek. Ignoring her cousins, she prowled along towards the rhubarb patch, seemingly aimless and intent on nothing in particular. Then, as she neared the fence, she raised her wet and dirty face and I knew she saw me. At that moment I slipped, embedding splinters from the rough wood into my hands and knees. Falling backwards, I came to rest in the sea of stingers, and lay there for a moment to absorb the enormity of my injuries before moving. There would be no Brownies for me tonight, my mother would have me convalescing on the settee. Just as well, as I was losing interest in the 'I promise to do my best' stuff and was rubbish at getting badges anyway.

# A Quiet Time In Carmarthenshire
### By Graham Watkins

'Rural Carmarthenshire has always been an idyllic, rustic paradise where time moves slowly, dictated by the seasons,' said the website. 'Where autumn follows summer and spring bringing new life to the fields, following the dark months of winter. In the heart of Carmarthenshire, nestling in the Towy Valley beneath the Brecon Beacons, sits the small town of Llangadog. First appearances are of a sleepy village, a place where motorists drive slowly around the dog, sleeping in the road outside the Red Lion - where locals, with time to spare, stop to gossip in the Post Office and the butcher next door knows every customer by name. A quiet tranquil backwater.'

A quiet tranquil backwater. That, if truth be known, was the reason I booked the holiday cottage; to escape and relax, away from my manic life. It was the picture of the dog lounging in the road that clinched it.

The cottage was small and sparsely furnished. The armchair by the fire had been well used. The sort of chair to doze in with your head resting against the high back. The arm had been patched with a square of faded green material. Dead people's furniture, my father would have called it.

A light drizzle had started to fall. The sky was heavy with dark brooding clouds. I unloaded the car, lit the wood burner and settled in for the afternoon. Ignoring the website warning of limited mobile coverage, I checked my phone for messages. Nothing, not one bar and the cottage had no wifi. I was alone, cut adrift from the world.

My electronic umbilical cord severed. London, my office, the people I called my friends removed by an impenetrable ether.

When I woke the cottage was almost dark, the only light a dim red glow from the fire. I checked my watch, half past seven. My neck ached and a foul taste filled my mouth. I gulped down a glass of water, grabbed my coat and went outside. A gust of icy wind chilled my bones and stung my eyes. A fine spray of rain, like a mist, soaked my face and ran down my neck. I pulled my collar up and walked quickly along the road, past the churchyard filled with, slate headstones and Victorian monuments. Ahead I could see a lamp above an open door, beckoning. I could hear laughter and a murmur of conversation. A woman laughed. The door was open and a ray of brightness flooded out. Beside the door, a granite mounting stone, polished by a thousand rider's boots, shimmered in the wet light. I went in.

The bar of the Red Lion was crowded with drinkers. The place was hot and had the air of a party, of friends letting their hair down, gossiping, telling jokes and flirting.

I pushed my way to the bar. 'A pint of bitter please.'

The barman pointed to the pumps. 'Which one?'

'Which one is local?'I asked.

'Try the Cwrw. That's what I drink,' said a man next to me.

I watched the barman pull the pint. The beer was warm with a distinct hoppy taste, refreshing and comforting. I moved away from the bar and looked for somewhere to sit. All the tables were full except one. In the far corner, beside the window, an old man, reading a newspaper, was sitting at the table. He was wearing a flat cap, a shabby tweed jacket with leather arm patches and a black waistcoat. A farmer, I guessed.

I made my way over to him. 'Do you mind if I sit here?'

'Please yourself,' he replied without looking up from the paper.

It was then that I saw the Collie under the table. I eased a chair over the dog and tried to sit down but there was no space for my legs.

'Get over,' growled the old man and shoved the dog with his foot. He folded the newspaper and slipped it into his jacket pocket. 'You're not from round here?'

'No. I'm from London.'

He removed his cap and scratched his balding head as if carefully considering my answer. 'London.... Yes, yes,' he replied and replaced his cap. 'Holidays is it?'

'Just a couple of days. A short break to get away.'

He nodded. There was an awkward silence. '...I went to Swansea once. Terrible place. All those people.'

I pictured him wandering around a city and smiled. 'Have you ever gone back?'

He slowly shook his head.

'So you prefer things nice and quiet. Llangadog does seem a sleepy place.'

'Nice and quiet! I could tell you a tale or two about Llangadog,' replied the old man and gently tapped the side of his empty glass.

A pint of beer for some stories seemed a fair trade. I went to the bar and returned with two drinks.

The old man took a mouthful. 'We had a murder here in 2004. In this very pub.' He raised his eyebrows.

Now, he had my full attention. 'Really? Where?'

'I was sitting right here, in the bar, when it happened. He was mad, you see, besotted by a younger woman.'

'Who was he?'

'William Davies. He walked into the bar with a shotgun and pointed it at Caroline Evans. She worked here. He was 59 and she was only 27. Pretty girl too. She was six months pregnant and wanted nothing to do with him. He shouted, 'I'll blow your brains out and then shoot myself. We'll go together.' No one moved or said a word. You could hear the clock in the hall ticking as they stared at each other. Then Ben here,' he pointed to the dog, 'growled. He knew something was terribly wrong.'

'Did he shoot her?'

The old man took another sip of his drink. 'The police confiscated his shotgun and charged him with threatening to kill.'

'But you said there was a murder. You said he was going to blow her brains out and then shoot himself.'

'And so I did.' The old man drained his glass, wiped his mouth with the back of his hand and smiled at me. 'It's a wet night. A whiskey to warm my bones.'

I went to the bar again.


'A psychiatrist said Davies was depressed but he was no danger to anyone else. The police dropped the charge of threatening to kill but, in case the psychiatrist was wrong, they kept his gun.'

It wasn't the ending I had expected. 'So no one got killed?' I felt a mixture of relief and ghoulish disappointment.

The old man leaned forward as if to share a secret. His stale breath repelled me but I had to hear.

'He stole a shotgun from a neighbour and came back.' The old man's eyes stared straight into mine. 'He did it. Blew her brains out, just as he said he would, then killed himself.'

I sat back, away from the old man's malodorous face and took a deep breath.

'A barmaid found both bodies when she came to work.'

We sat watching customers at the bar.

A stout man in a Wales rugby shirt was telling a joke. An appreciative group gathered around him. '... then I found someone was accessing my online bank account. I turned detective and found a man from New Zealand I thought was the thief. I confronted the Kiwi but he was slapping his arms and legs and sticking his tongue out. Do you know why?' Rugby shirt paused.... 'He was a haka.'

Groans and laughter greeted the punch-line.

The old man rubbed a hole in the condensation on the window. 'It's raining again just like in 1987. I remember the rain didn't stop for weeks.'

He was talking quietly, as if to himself. I leaned forward to catch what he was saying.

'Ben and I were moving some cattle by the river at Glanrhydsaeson when the accident happened. The river was about to burst its bank and flood the fields. Do you see? We had to move the cows to higher ground.'

'What happened?'

The old man turned and faced me. He looked sad. 'The railway bridge collapsed pitching the early train into the river. The driver and three passengers drowned in the Towy that morning. I helped recover the bodies from the water.'

I contemplated what he said. Murder and a suicide in the pub and before that a rail disaster. Not what I'd expected to hear in sleepy Llangadog.

'Are you hungry?' asked the old man. He was smiling. 'They do some excellent bar meals here.' He tapped his empty glass. 'Let's eat.'

I'd had nothing since breakfast and was hungry. It would be rude to sit and eat without inviting the old man to join me and, to be honest, I was enjoying his company. I fetched a menu and more drinks from the bar while he went to the toilet. Ben didn't stir from his place under the table.

'It isn't all death and destruction,' said the old man. 'Did I tell you I once had a dairy farm of my own?'

I watched him cut a piece of steak and sneak it under the table to his dog. 'No. You said you used to move cows.'

'Before then, I farmed at Gwynfe. Had 36 milking cows. The tanker used to collect the milk every morning and bring it down to The Creamery here in Llangadog. Then, they introduced milk quotas and we knew we had to do something.'

'Milk quotas, when was this?'

'1984. The Minister of Agriculture, Mr. Jopling, himself came to explain.' He stabbed to air in front of me with a finger. 'It was our chance to show him a thing or two. Two thousand of us showed up on our tractors. We blocked all the roads trapping the minister for hours and released hundreds of gallons of milk in protest. It was a grand day but I knew the end of milk farming was coming. It was time for Ben and me to do something else.' He shoved a mushroom into his mouth and chewed as he spoke. 'I was right. They closed The Creamery in 2005.'

Did the old man just say it was time to do something else in 1984? I did a quick mental sum. That was thirty-two years ago. He would have been alive then, but the dog? It must have been a different dog or was the Cwrw effecting my hearing and arithmetic? But then, did it really matter? I felt relaxed. So what if the old man got his dates wrong. He was entertaining and, for the first time in weeks, I felt relaxed and a bit drunk. My break in the country was doing some good.

The barman came over and cleared our plates away.

'Gangsters,' said the old man, 'You have them in London don't you? Krays, Richardsons. I've read about them in the papers.'

'The Krays are dead but we do still have gangs in London,' I replied.

'Ben can smell them, you know; gangsters, he can smell them.'

I looked down at the dog asleep at my feet. 'You have gangsters here?'

The old man nodded. 'The first one was called Malcolm Heaysman, he turned up in 1971 and bought Godrewaun Cottage in the village. Ben didn't like him. He would snarl every time he saw the man and....'

'Just a minute. How old is your dog?'

'I don't really know.' He shrugged. 'I didn't have him as a puppy. As I was saying, he didn't like the man. We were in the lane one morning when a car pulled up. There were two men inside, strangers I'd never seen before. Ben went up to the car and then did something odd, something he'd never done before; he came and sat behind me, almost cowering. They asked if a single Englishman, an old friend of theirs, had recently moved into the village. Oh yes, I said and told them about the man doing up Godrewaun Cottage. They drove off. That's the last I saw of them.'

'What happened?'

'Heaysman was beaten to death by the two men who parked their car and walked across the fields to his house. The police said he was a gangster from Islington, killed to settle an old score.'

I got up and made my way through the hall to the toilet. The Cwrw was stronger than I'd expected. The hall clock chimed the half hour as I returned. Was it really only eight thirty? I wasn't sure. We'd eaten a meal and I thought I'd been listening to the old man for hours. How many drinks had we consumed? Five, six, more; again I wasn't sure. How old was Ben? I no longer cared. It didn't matter. Nothing mattered.

Something had changed in the bar. It took me a moment to understand what exactly. The air was thick with cigarette smoke and the old man in the corner was smoking a pipe. I watched him tamp down the tobacco and strike a match.

He dropped the match into an ashtray on the table. 'Did I tell you about the fire?'

'No. What fire?'

The old man leaned back and blew a smoke ring in the air. 'It was in 1953 or was it 52? I'm not sure now. Anyway, my neighbours, at Glanrhyd Meilock, Mr. and Mrs Williams and their children were in bed when a fire started in the kitchen.' The smoke ring had fallen and was settling on the table. He waved it away. 'They escaped down the stairs and out the front door. Mrs Williams told me there so much smoke they had to go down the stairs, backwards, on their bellies. Then she remembered her mother.'

'Her mother. Whose mother?'

The old man raised an eyebrow. 'I just told you, her mother. Mrs Williams' mother, the blind 80 year-old invalid, was asleep in a downstairs room, behind the kitchen. Mrs Williams went back into the house. Her husband tried to stop her. You see, the house was in flames. She told me the fire had spread across much of the kitchen. She crawled across the floor and dragged her mother out. Both women survived but Mrs Williams remained in hospital for some time with serious burns to her back. I used to visit her every week. Of course, I didn't take Ben. Dogs aren't allowed in hospitals.' The old man puffed his pipe, coughed, cleared his throat and sniffed loudly. 'The farmhouse was completely destroyed. We had to do something. I started a collection.' He sat up and pointed to his chest. 'People were very kind. The village collected enough money to completely rebuild the house within a year, imagine that, and Mrs Williams was awarded the British Empire Medal for her bravery.'

Thinking of Mrs Williams crawling across a smoke-filled kitchen, I peered through the smoky gloom of the bar and noticed, the man wearing the red rugby shirt had left. There was something else, all the women who had been there, earlier in the evening, were gone. The room was darker and for some reason, I could not fathom, the landlord had turned off the beer pump's neon signs. I turned back. A youth, I hadn't seen before, was refilling my beer from a large metal jug. 'Thanks,' I said and picked the glass up by its handle.

'Ben did his bit in the war,' said the old man.

I started to laugh. The old man was a fool to be humoured. 'Ben. Which war was that? The Boer War.' I sniggered. 'Was he in the army or the navy?'

'No.' The old man looked offended. 'We were on the mountain. Ben was barking. He'd found a dead man in a gully.'

I stopped smiling. 'A body, who was he?'

'There was three pounds ten shillings in his wallet which I was very glad of and an identity card.'

'You took his money? You stole from a dead man?'

'He wasn't going to spend it, was he? The old man shrugged. 'His name was Sergeant Jones. He'd baled out of a damaged Lancaster bomber. We found the parachute where he came down. The poor sod crawled three miles with a broken leg before dying.'

I'd heard enough. The old man with bad breath was a thief, a liar and a sponger. I'd been buying him drinks all evening. It was time to get back to the cottage. What was the time? I held up my arm to look at my watch. It wasn't there. 'Have you stalen my witch?' I tried again, speaking more slowly. 'Have you stolen my watch?'

The old man was lighting his pipe from a candle on the table. He shook his head.

'What's the candle for? Has the power gone off?'

'Stalen witches you say, power gone off. What do you mean?'

I wanted to explain but the words would not come. I took a mouthful of ale from the tankard in front of me.

'I used to drink with William Powell,' said the old man. 'He wasn't a friend but he had a few bob and was always willing to buy a round for anyone who would listen to his bragging.'

I concentrated on watching the old man's mouth. 'What sort of stories?'

'He lived at Glanaraeth Mansion. One night, when he'd had a good drink, he told me about his trial for killing a servant girl. He was accused of pushing her out of an upstairs window. The jury found him not guilty and he told me why.'

Tired as I was, I wanted to know more. 'Go on.'

'Said he tried to seduce her. He liked the ladies, you see, but she refused to submit. He knew the jury would convict so he bribed them and walked from the courtroom a free man.'

My eyelids were closed when something knocked against my leg. Ben jumped up and growled. A man was spreading sawdust across the bare floorboards with a broom.

'Lay down,' ordered the old man. 'There was a witness, a servant boy who mysteriously vanished.' He covered his mouth with the back of his hand to hide the words. 'Some say Powell killed him and chopped up the body.'

'What happened to him?'

'The boy? Nobody knows.'

No, I mean Powell. What happened to him?'

The old man grinned. 'He built a house next door to this pub and used it to entertain different women. When Bill Williams, he was a draper from Llandovery, discovered his wife had been to Powell's house he was mad with anger but he wasn't the only one wanting revenge on Powell. A gang of them went to Powell's mansion and murdered him.'

'Sounds like he deserved it,' said sleepily.

'The stupid men left footprints in the snow and were soon caught, all except Williams. He escaped to France.'

I collected my wits and asked the question that I knew he couldn't answer. 'When was this man you used to drink with murdered?'

'What do you mean. You must have read about the murder. It was in all the papers. It was last January.'

'January, yes, no, I mean what year. Tell me the year.'

The old man looked at me as if I was an idiot. 'This year of course 1768. When did you think?'

I stood up and tried to focus. 'You're a liar. That was two hundred and fifty years ago.'

The old man drew the newspaper from his jacket pocket. 'So I lie do I?' He handed the news sheet to me. 'Here at the top.'

I sat down and read the headline. 'Two hanged for Powell Murder, other assassins turn king's evidence to cheat gallows.'

'What's the date?' demanded the old man. 'Tell me the date on the paper.'

It was in small print in the corner of the page. '11th day of September 1768.'

I woke and sat up in the chair. A ray of sunshine illuminated the cottage. I felt awful. The beer monster was taking its revenge for my heavy night. As the details of the evening slowly emerged I realised how ridiculous it all was. I must have been very drunk. How did I get back from the Red Lion? I didn't remember that part of the evening but the old man; I couldn't get him out of my mind. Who was he and where did he get all the ridiculous stories from?

I splashed some water on my face and cleaned my teeth. It was nearly mid-day, the pub should be open by now. I walked back through Llangadog, past the church, and on, along Church Street to the Red Lion. A sheepdog was asleep in the road.

'Ben,' I called. 'Here boy.'

The dog stood up, eyed me with distain and trotted away.

I tried the door of the Red Lion. It was locked. A man emerged from the post office opposite.

'What time does the pub open?' I asked.

'It doesn't,' he replied. 'The place has been closed for months.'

I looked through the window. The table where I sat with the old man was in the corner but it was covered in rubbish, discarded cans of pop, sandwich wrappers and an old newspaper. I tried to read the date on the paper but the print was faded. I stepped back across the road and saw a 'For Sale' board fixed from an upstairs window. I began to walk back, towards the cottage and had only taken a few steps when a dog barked behind me. The collie had returned to the Red Lion and was sitting in the road. I'm not sure if the dog's bark was telling me to but I looked up and there, above the doorway, was

38

William Powell's name carved in a slate panel. I was standing outside the house he built before he was murdered.

# The Last Second
By Colin R Parsons

It was something to do with the rotation of the earth, or some scientific equation, but as we rolled into twenty-seventeen, there was an extra second added to the clock - a small, insignificant fragment of time that didn't mean anything to anyone really. But I believe that that was a turning point in history. And it got me thinking.

What if that second took us back in time, instead of forward? What if that puny little second altered our way of thinking? What if that small piece of nothingness took us to a different place entirely – an adjacent life to the one we already have? To one person, that second made one hell of a difference.

This is what happened to Gerry Dean…

The last seconds of 2016 ticked away. It was almost midnight. The clock on the telly displayed 59 minutes and 57 seconds, 58 seconds… Gerry eagerly sat there with a party popper in his left hand, and the string that dangled down in his right. 59 seconds appeared on the clock, and then… nothing! The digital clock face had stopped at 23.59.59! Gerry sat there not quite knowing what to do. And he also noticed that not only had the clock frozen on that fifty-ninth second, but the television picture had too! He'd been watching the show all night just for that moment.

All his anticipation and the adrenalin suddenly drifted away and he felt cheated. He looked at the party popper with disgust and tossed it on the table. He realised with sadness that it was the very first time ever, in his entire life, he'd missed the rolling in of the New Year. It was gone! It had happened without him.

He slumped back into his grimy, moth-eaten armchair and scratched the stubble on his chin. He let out a long, gushing sigh. Truth be told, he was devastated. The old man grabbed for his celebratory whisky and swallowed it down, anyway, in one, quick gulp. The hard liquor bit deep into his throat, and he winced with satisfaction. He sat and pondered - the waft of his smelly slippers mixing in with the rest of the stench around him.

'It's New Year's Day,' he said ominously, and rolled his head from side to side, letting out another gush of air from his mouth. He looked at the telly once again but that was still stuck in the same position. There was obviously a problem with the digital-box or something – he didn't know.

'Hey, wait a minute,' he slurred, as if talking to someone in the room, 'why aren't the bells from the church ringing in the New Year?' That was strange, and got him thinking. 'Why weren't there people celebrating in the street?' It always happened after the midnight hour - with screaming and shouting going on until at least one or two in the morning.

He decided to go and take look out of his window and see what was - or wasn't - happening. Gerry Dean got up from his chair and dragged himself the few steps to the bay window – mindful of all the rubbish on the floor. He pulled back the grotty, orange curtains and peered into the blackness. There was nothing to see, literally.

'What on earth was happening?' There were no street lights – it was really dark out there. Gerry instantly realised that it must have been a blackout of some sort a power-cut maybe? 'The street lights should be on, so there's got to be an electrical fault,' he murmured. And he assumed that was why the telly froze up. Maybe, also, why the church bells weren't ringing. Then a thought crossed his mind. If it was a blackout, how were his living room lights still on, and the telly still working? This really didn't make any sense.

So, he decided to investigate for himself and go outside. He turned away from the window and focussed his thoughts on where he'd put his torch. It would, hopefully, be in the small drawer next to his armchair. He gave himself a wry smile – 'A place for everything, and everything in its place,' he said with pride, which was ironic because his house was a tip. He may have had a place for everything, but to look at his house - it was piled up to the hilt, with... nothing at all really. Gerry was a hoarder of rubbish.

It was at that point that he glanced at the drawer next to his chair and remembered - that was where he'd left it - he nodded to himself contentedly. Then something told him to look at his armchair. And that was a mistake! When he did, he almost choked! His eyes widened and he suddenly found it hard to breathe. He could feel the nerves tighten in his stomach. His whole body trembled, like the start of an earthquake.

There was someone sitting in his chair! Gerry was standing on the only clear spot on the floor, between a pile of newspapers and a collection of empty beer bottles. His brown eyes were unblinking – his mouth completely dry. He could smell the stale alcohol of his own breath, mixed with many other dank odours that filled the room. For a moment, he thought he was going to cry, but just about managed to hold it back. What was happening to him on this weird night? It was his own image no, not an image, he was actually sitting there.

'H-how can th-is be?' he stuttered, his voice trembling. He was confused; maybe this was a drunken illusion! He knew he'd probably had a good drink that evening. Well, it was New Year's Eve, but that never mattered to him. And anyway, he knew in his heart-of-hearts that whenever he drank too much, which was all the time, he was mostly immune to the effects. His body had got used to it, he supposed. How bad had his drinking got? His memories were quite fuzzy at this point.

Gerry squinted at the second Gerry Dean, perched in the armchair as if welded to the furniture. The other Gerry Dean was grizzled and old, and dirty, overweight and disgusting, and seeing himself from the outside was terrifying. 'This can't be me,' he said. He couldn't believe it. 'This is all wrong. This is not me,' he repeated, and refused to believe it. 'I like a drink, but surely not to this extent?'

So, he took a look at his own body while he stood there. He lifted his hands to his face – palms up. He was young and his hands were white, and the skin was fresh and new. His nemesis sitting in that chair over there had mottled skin and sunken eyes, with a nose redder than Rudolph's. What did this mean? Gerry turned to the tarnished mirror in the corner of his grimy room – the cobwebs were draped over the frame, like an eerie Halloween prop.

'Oh, Jesus.' He almost cried at the reflection. He looked so handsome, tall and healthy, with bright eyes. What was he doing in this dirty, rundown shack? How was he old and decrepit over there, and young and vivacious over here? It didn't make any sense. The answers he was looking for were outside the house. He was sure of it something pulled at him to look out there. He needed to go right now.

He tried to make his way to the front door, but found it hard to actually move his limbs. His whole body felt numb, and when he attempted to move, it was like trying to wade through a thick layer of custard. This was all so very, very strange, almost dream-like. The young Gerry, after a slow and tedious push, eventually made it. When he got there, it all looked as drab as the living room – the passage and the door itself. The whole house was a complete shambles, exactly the opposite of how he used to be. So how hadn't he made a success of his life? The answers, he knew, were beyond that door. All he had to do now was twist the Yale lock… and simply open the door to find out what was calling to him. But he was scared.

He glanced back at the living room and saw the same tired old face in front of the goggle box. That was the same person who'd wasted his whole life just staring at a small square picture frame of moving images. The young Gerry turned to the door again, and reached out. He didn't even have to touch the latch and the door swept open. He edged back a little for fear of being confronted by something. But there, in front of his eyes, was the same black mass he'd seen through the window. He found that he couldn't see through it, or into the background. There were no shapes to depict the street and buildings. In fact, Gerry couldn't see anything beyond the edges of the darkness. What was this? He reached out again to touch the mysterious blackened wall, when a really weird thing happened… it turned into a giant picture show, a huge television screen.

But the images portrayed his life from a child and showed his history in one long movie reel. The young Gerry stood with eyes filled with tears. He could finally see how he'd gone from a young, successful entrepreneur, to a dirty, alcohol-ridden recluse. He witnessed the love of his life, 'Jenny', enter his world, and take everything she could from him, before moving on to the next victim. There was no love, only greed. He saw his own decline, from a highly-respected businessman to someone who looked for answers at the bottom of a bottle. And why he'd fallen further and further into the depths of hell. This was a lot to take in and the young Gerry couldn't understand why this had been shown to him. He now remembered what had taken place in his life. So, was this a second chance, or something more sinister?

The visual picture finally faded back to its original black space and Gerry was left standing in his hallway, with a whole lot of doubt and despair. What was he supposed to do now? As the door closed again, so the young Gerry's vision faded.

The clock on the television eventually flashed back to life and struck the hour of midnight. In the background, the bells of St Mary's chimed merrily, bringing in the New Year. Joy and laughter rang out from the streets, beyond his window. But the grizzled old man in the chair sat stiff and lifeless – still holding the party popper in his left hand, and the string in his right. Gerry's dark, milky eyes were wide open. The tears of a long lost memory had rolled down and dried in clean lines on his dirty cheeks. Time rolled on, as it normally does for everybody else, to bring in the fresh New Year. But Gerry Dean's life stopped there and then, at that one extra second, and he took all the heartache with him to the next world. This all happened in that one last second.

# Grey Blanket
By Ciaran O Connell

He looks dangerous as you weave your way past him. You can feel the heat of his anger. Don't look down, you tell yourself. But the smell, that familiar smell, that's what reaches into you. A sudden wave of nausea floods your throat.

'Bloody junkie,' the young lad ahead of you mutters.

Has the beggar heard him? Will he think it was you? Keep looking ahead. But you can't help it. You look down. It's a filthy face. There's a large scab on his left cheekbone. He catches your eye. He lifts an eyebrow and offers you a near toothless grin then lowers his head again.

He's wrapped in so many sweaters you have no idea if he is a bear or a stick insect lost in an oversized cocoon, the tramp, the beggar, the homeless guy. The very words sit sheepishly inside your head. His hands are fists clenched tight in his lap, as he repeats his hopeless ask. He speaks to the floor. You can't make out the words. But you get the message. Why don't you stop to check if he is okay or needs some help? You are in hurry. That's why. He's not my problem, you tell yourself. The truth is that smell has set off too many alarm bells in your head. You've got to get away.

You are irritated by where he has placed himself. Like a scruffy Buddha, he sits, cross-legged on the floor of the ticket hall. He leans against the maroon tiles next to the exit tunnel. But he sticks out, blocking half the tunnel and forcing everyone to take steps to avoid tripping up over him.

It's been two months since you last made this journey. The whole morning has been planned out for you. First you must to get through your meeting with Rob, the Managing Director. You need to reassure him that you are okay, ready to get back into the thick of things. You need to be on top of your game for that. You speed onward, leaving the beggar behind but carrying with you a trickle of shame. Before this can lead to a flood of unwanted memories you divert it down into the depths, shut the trapdoor and step up your pace.

You've made it past him. Great. A flash of daylight calls. Head down, you march through the dim tunnel, its tiles shouting Jack the Ripper. After twenty or so uphill strides you are faced with a pedestrian T-junction. The sign on the wall directs you - left for Madam Tussaud's, and right for Great Portland Street tube station.

You turn right, up the steep steps. One sharp turn at the top and there you are, on the south side of a noisy road. To your right, tall black railings imprison a parade of evergreen shrubs planted to shield the secluded garden of a perfect Georgian Crescent from the curious. You wonder what the garden looks like, and who uses it. You picture a past where starched nannies chatted to each other as they slowly pushed prams. You could walk its circumference in less than five minutes.

But you don't. You walk in the direction you had planned to. Your heart is beating faster than normal. You try again to shove the memories back down. It was his smell that set them loose. Images of that night begin to flash about inside your head.

You turn back for a final look at the little park. That's when you first spot him, the man from the tube station, the beggar. You search for a less demeaning word. Nothing comes to mind. There's nobody else on the pavement and he is walking towards you. In the moment before you jerk your head back, you notice that he is carrying a grey blanket draped across his right shoulder. And he has a dog, a stocky dog, on a rope. Is he looking at you? Don't be so stupid, you tell yourself. Though you do quicken your pace a little.

You reach the traffic lights as they change to green. Why would you think he was following you? You weren't the one who swore at him. Another memory flares up in your head. The sound of harsh swearing and men laughing; and the smell, that sickening smell. It seems to be getting stronger. You're sweating. You take a deep breath and walk on.

Now you are leaving the elegant buildings behind and you come to the bronze bust of John F. Kennedy. It's a good likeness. He sits on his man-high plinth in a cream coloured alcove. He is guarded on either side by two cherry trees. He was one of the good guys, you tell yourself. He still got shot though. You've seen it on television hundreds of times, and always in slow motion. This close up view of the dead president somehow slows the pace of your journey. Or rather the sense of the pace, for you still walk to your slightly hurried beat. Not a stroll, not quite a full-on hurry, but with intent.

Marylebone Road is a wide road. Even at this early hour it's an incessant torrent of black cabs, double-decker buses, motorbikes, vans, cars and coaches; all woven together by a continuous braid of cyclists, some daring, some panicky. You're past the tube station now. You turn into a side street. The noise drops to a hum. You stare through the windows of a Volvo dealership at giant luxury cars.

The memory of your encounter with the homeless guy at the tube station has lost its guilty coating. But the strong smell of his stale sweat still catches in your throat. It drags you back to that night on the South Bank. There were three of them, all in their early twenties, and so full of hate. They had long ratty hair. Like this guy - dull, heavily matted and tangled.

You're breathing heavily now. You want to take a quick look back. He has probably carried on down Marylebone Road. Or, perhaps he stopped and is trying his luck outside Great Portland Street station. You want to be sure. You're afraid to turn your head.

You are another fifty metres down before you finally give in to the urge, and turn. The street is empty. He's not there. A deep breath is so refreshing. You smile to yourself and enjoy the warmth of relief. What a fool you've been. You stand and look up at a clear blue sky. The air is clean and crisp. You take another look back, just to be sure. That's when you see the dog's head. It has popped out from behind a pillar. There is a pounding in your chest. You look closer, and then you spot it, the grey blanket. Is he hiding? Why would he be hiding? Maybe he is looking at the big flash cars as you did?

You move on, thankful he hasn't seen that you turned back to look. Though the dog certainly has. You're not hiding your panic now. It's beginning to take charge. You know that this is not good. You swallow a lump that has found its way into your throat. You're arguing with yourself now.

'This is broad daylight.'

' So?'

' There are lots of people about.'

There were lots of people on the South Bank that night. But not where you were walking, not in that underpass. By now, you have turned the corner into the shabby end of Warren Street. Across the road sits a tiny Moroccan cafe that has occasionally had your lunchtime business. It is closed at this hour, and besides, you're in no mood for food. Outside the bikers' café, the couriers in their leathers, with helmets removed, stare at you as you hurry by. You don't notice. Soon you reach the North West corner of Fitzroy Square. You're being an idiot, you tell yourself. It's just a coincidence - a coincidence that he is heading in the same direction as you. You repeat this, like a futile mantra.

Don't be so silly, you whisper. But you're not really listening. You're back on that concrete walkway frozen in fear. They keep kicking. You hear, once more, the dull crumpled thuds as their boots find their target again and again. And the smell... oh that smell, you want to throw up.

You're speeding up again. You want to turn and take another look. You're desperate to check if he is still there. But you hold back. What would he do if he saw you looking back at him? What if it is just coincidence – which, of course, it is, you remind the panicking person inside your head. He's got a dog. It looked like a pit bull terrier. So you keep walking. He's just another homeless guy, you tell yourself. Nothing like those others. Just a lad down on his luck. You wish, suddenly, you had given him some change. Too late now.

You are walking too fast. You know it. You try to slow down. It's no good. You've got to keep moving. What if he is gaining on you? You don't even know if he is following you. As you pass a removal van parked outside the Croatian Embassy, you have an idea.

I might just look back to see what's inside the van, just out of curiosity. You try out this self-delusion on your rational half. You buy into it. After you have passed the end of the van you count six steps. Then, still walking, and trying not to slow your pace, you turn your head and take a look. The van's back doors are open. Two men are folding up those grey woollen removal blankets and stacking them in a neat pile near the open doors. The rest of the van is a big empty space. You feel a tightening in your chest. Go on! Do it. You let your eyes shift to beyond the van. There it is, the other grey blanket. It's getting closer. Turn back. Keep walking.

Was he looking at me? You can't be sure. He was scowling. You are convinced you saw a scowl. By now you have reached the south side of the square. In the days before, you would have enjoyed the crunch of your feet on the square's gravel. You would have been filled with curiosity about all the people you pass. You would have noticed the woman escorting two young schoolgirls, the two men removing scaffolding from a building. You would have wondered if the woman was the girls' mother, or perhaps an au pair, what will the building look like with the scaffolding down. A young man passes in front of you on a Boris bike, an overstuffed black briefcase strapped to the basket. Is he a trainee solicitor, perhaps an account manager in one of the ad agencies on Charlotte Street? You don't ask yourself any of these questions.

You have made it to the south east corner, and you pass the railed off statue of General Francisco de Miranda. He stands close up against the brick wall of an elegant townhouse, all bronze and larger than life with his sword held aloft. On the railings, a plaque reminds you that he had lived there in eighteen something or other. He stares out belligerently, daring you to challenge his right to occupy that space. You have often promised yourself that you would stop and read the inscription. Today is not a day for that. By now you are into Charlotte Street. As you pass the Saatchi building you risk another quick look. You can't see him. You stop walking. You scan the street and the square. He's not there. There's no grey blanket. There's no dog.

You take a deep breath and let it out slowly. What a paranoid fool you have been. It was a coincidence. You drop your speed, taking another quick look back, just to be sure. No, he's definitely gone. Still, your heart is pounding. You are swamped by that familiar flood of guilt. You did nothing. Nothing to help that poor girl. You stood in the shadows and watched as they kicked the life out of her. Why did you do nothing? You know why. You don't want to hear why. You might have saved her. You shake your head. No! You don't want these thoughts.

You want the sneering voice inside your head to shut up. You dig out your headphones, and plug yourself into your iphone. You turn the volume up high. Now you are marching to the beat of Ray Lamontagne.

You turn into Percy Street. Standing outside your office block, you know you are the first to arrive and will have to open up the studio on the second floor. You dig through the outer pocket of your rucksack and drag out the keys. You punch in the entry code, lean over and push the glass door open. Mr American Lamontagne is still singing his heart out. 'Trouble....', his rough forty fags a day voice drags the word out as he sings, 'trouble…, trouble, trouble.'.

But he can't drown out the sound of their boots sinking into her limp body. He can't obliterate the look on her parents' faces as you give your evidence to the coroner. You run up the stairs. You are on the second floor now. You keep climbing, past your office, on up.

And here you are on the roof. You can't get the smell out of your nostrils. You take a deep breath but it's no good. It's suffocating you.

'Are you alright mate?' It's another rough edged voice. You look down. Grey blanket and his dog are standing in the street. You're standing on the ledge.

# The Journey
By Graham Watkins

I stop the car, get out and look down the valley. Far below me, stretching toward the distant Rocky Mountains is Kamloops Lake, a ribbon of blue water. Paddle steamers once plied the lake carrying lumber and supplies to the mining camps, iron rails and sleepers for the new railroad. Gold fever gripped British Columbia. Places like Frazer River where fine, flour-like, gold was being panned and Bakerville, a wild shanty of a town in the Cariboo, built on stories of golden nuggets waiting to be picked from the ground, fed men's dreams. They too travelled west on the sternwheelers, each searching for their own Eldorado. Jack Cooper was also a passenger but his journey was east in 1867 and his bags were full of gold. He struck pay-dirt on the Frazer River at Lillooet. His claim was the most profitable in the valley and, with enough gold to live like a king, he sold the claim and returned to civilisation.

A banshee whistle echoing across the valley interrupts my thoughts of Jack. A train is moving, snail like, along the side of the lake. Two huge engines are pulling. I count the trucks; seventy-five then a third engine and yet more trucks. Shipping containers stacked two high, oil tankers, livestock carriages all haphazardly mixed together. I do a mental sum; one hundred and thirty tons per railway truck plus six hundred tons for the engines. Over fifteen thousand tons is snaking its way slowly through the valley. The paddle steamers, that brought the materials to build the Canadian Pacific railroad, delivered their own doom. The rails, sleepers and rolling stock providing faster, more efficient and less expensive transport. The lake is silent. The steamers long since beached and broken up.

I return to the car and continue west along the highway, through hills and valleys, past quarries and cattle ranches. Juggernauts chug, tortoise like, up the hills, hazards flashing. I overtake and reach the top. Descending, I'm tailgated by the same trucks. They've caught up. They thunder past, desperate to gain momentum for the next roller coaster climb. The wild game of leap frog continues for miles, until they are gone. The road is clear. There are no trees, no cattle only desert, a barren tundra of scrub and dust. Sweat is dripping from me. I close the sunroof, turn on the air conditioning and drive another fifty miles until I reach a valley.

'Cooper Creek,' says the billboard. 'An oasis in the desert.' I pull off the highway and drive slowly along Main Street.

A sign flickers, 'Clean rooms. Discounts for seniors.' The motel reception is empty. There's a phone on the counter. I pick it up.

'What?' demands a woman's voice.

'I'd like a room.'

'What kinda room?'

'A bedroom for tonight.' It seems a reasonable answer.

'Queen, double queen, king, family room. What kind?'

I don't reply.

'Ok. Stay there. I'll come down.'

A fifty something woman appears, unkempt and sweaty. She stinks of tobacco and stale alcohol. She hands me a key. 'Where ya from?'

'The UK.'

'UK, nice. Your room's one ten. No pets, no smoking in the room, that's the law. Park outside your room nose in. Checkout's before eleven or you'll be charged an extra night.'

Room one hundred and ten is at the back of the motel beside the remains of a swimming pool; a cracked concrete pit half filled with brown water. A faded life ring hangs from a rusting frame. 'No diving,' says the sign. Wooden stairs in front of my window lead to the upper floor. I unlock the door and push hard. The room is dark, tired and oven like. An air conditioning unit fills the top half of the window frame. I play with the controls. It gurgles into life, spraying me with dried leaves and dust. The compressor hums, vibrating against the window.

I leave my bag and head out to see what Cooper Creek has to offer. Walking along the street I cross a small bridge spanning the creek. It's a dry bed of rocks and gravel. The visitor's centre is the first building. It's barred and shuttered. A ripped red and yellow canopy stretches across the front of the building. Beneath it a life size tableau of painted figures. Marlon Brando clad in black leather, Marilyn Munroe white dress billowing, James Dean scowling over his shoulder and other stars, whose names I've long ago forgotten.

The liquor store's neon light beckons. A man behind the counter is reading a newspaper. He looks up. The half empty wooden shelves sag with age. I can smell the dust and decay. I take a bottle of whiskey to the counter and pay.

'Where ya from,' asks the man. 'You want a bag for that?'

'I've driven from Jasper.' I nod.

'Jasper, nice. Hotter here, Huh?'

'Yes it is.'

He places the bottle in a brown paper bag. 'Yeah, hotter. You stayin at the motel?'

I nod again.

He leans forward. 'Watch out for the rattlers.' He sees I don't understand. 'Rattlesnakes, the creek is full of them. They get into the motel sometimes.' He grins. 'Check under the bed.'

Two doors along is Mario's Greek Taverna. I go in. The Taverna is empty. I see the plastic tablecloths, sachets of ketchup and mustard and plastic chairs and leave. Alongside Mario's is a pub. The bar is large with wooden chairs and tables. There's a raised dance floor near the door and two pool tables to one side. A silent ice hockey game is playing on the line of television screens above the bar. The players are fighting. Cowboy music plays in the background. A clutch of afternoon drinkers are seated at a table near the bar. They glance at me briefly and continue their conversation. The talk is loud, peppered with swearwords and drunken raucous laughter. I imagine the place late at night, packed with rowdy revellers, a bar room brawl, Chuck Norris using a pool cue to settle an argument with three men.

A waitress steps from behind the bar. She's young, overweight and her arms are black with tattoos of skulls, motorbikes, goths and gravestones. 'Table for one?' She leads me to a table and returns with iced water and a menu. 'You American?'

'I'm British,' I reply.

'British, nice. Can I get you a drink?'

I study the menu. 'I'll have a lager, sixteen ounce and a pepperoni pizza.'

'Sure. Extra cheese?'

'No thanks.'

'Fries?'

'No.'

'Nice. Right away.' She disappears through a door leading to Mario's Taverna to place my order.

There's a picture on the wall and a plaque. I go across to have a closer look. It's a sepia photograph of an old man dressed in a suit and a beaver skin hat. He looks stiff, holding his breath while the plate captures his image. A caption says, 'Jacob Cooper.' I study the plaque. So this is Jacob Cooper, Jack's father. I learn more. Jacob was a fur trapper who staked his claim to Cooper Creek in the 1840's. He traded with Indians and married Skaiya'm a Státimc Nation woman from Lillooet. Jacob called her Sarah after Abraham's wife in the Bible and said, like Abraham's Sarah, she was a princess. I remembered the story. Jack was their first son.

I return to my table. Beer, ketchup and cutlery are there. The drinkers are breaking up. Heading home. The door to Mario's opens. The waitress delivers my dinner with a flourish. The pizza is the size of a dustbin lid.

'Enjoy.' says the waitress.

'It's odd, don't you think?' I say. 'I'm in Canada, being served German beer in a pretend British pub, eating Italian food, cooked in a Greek restaurant.'

She pauses for a second. '... You want another beer?'

I'm in the motel room. I check under the bed and in the bathroom. There's no sign of rattlesnakes. The air conditioner has done its work but is vibrating noisily. The room is ice cold. I switch the machine off, open a window and pour a whiskey. I lay naked on the bed and consider the picture of Jacob. It must have been taken in his old age. So it was from here that the half breed, Jack, set out from to make his fortune in Lillooet. I wondered, did he walk the fifty miles or ride a horse. A puddle of sweat has collected in my navel. There are voices outside. Three men climb the stairs and enter the room above mine. I drift off.

I'm woken by a noise and bright white lights. A Ram pickup truck, engine throbbing, is outside my window. The engine stops. Two women step out. They're dressed in shirts and tight pants. One is sucking from a plastic cup with a straw. They go upstairs. Doors bang. There's laughter and muffled voices. They've joined the men. Again I sleep.

It's three o'clock and I'm awake. The bedroom is a furnace. The people in the room above me are copulating. The sex is vigorous and the women vocal. I turn on the air conditioner to drown the noise and cool the room, fetch a blanket from the chair and return to bed. My sleep is fitful. I dream of Jacob, Sarah and Jake, of how this place was before I came when the creek was filled with water, an oasis in the desert.

A door slams. Footsteps on the wooden stairs.

'Screw you,' shouts a woman outside my window. The truck starts. Headlamps illuminate the room. They gun the engine and are gone. A toilet flushes above me and then all I hear is the relentless drone of the air conditioner.

'How was your night?' asks the sweaty receptionist.
'My night, nice,' I reply.
'Where ya headed to today, somewhere nice?'
'Medicine Falls.'
'Medicine Falls, nice,' she says.

I reach Medicine Falls late in the morning. The waterfall pours cool clear water into Medicine Lake. The RV campground, a lush meadow beside the water, is full. Children are playing. Everything is prepared. The Potlatch has started. A field has been cleared for the festivities. The Státimc Nation have gathered for their annual gift giving feast. Men dressed in jeans and buckskin shirts are barbequing venison burgers. Women in Indian finery are serving at long tables.

They are making up for the years when the government banned such feasts, when Indian children were taken from their families and imprisoned in Catholic faith schools, when being an Indian was to be a savage with no rights, no land and no hope. Canadians of Chinese descent are here, too. celebrating their liberation from oppression, from the white man's cruelty. The Chinese also mined in Lilloet but not only for gold. Gold they said has no soul. They dug for a green treasure prized for its beauty in the Orient; jade.

Chief Hunting Bear, a giant of a man, is striding towards me. 'You came!' He smiles and pulls me towards him in a crushing hug. We gather on an area of dry earth. A fire burns in the centre as the

Státimc people arrange themselves in a large circle. Dancers in beaded blankets stand with their backs to the fire. The drummers start. A steady rhythmic sound. Dancers chant and sway from side to side. They gyrate, shuffling slowly around the circle. Hunting Bear sits. I stand behind him and wait to be admitted to the circle to become a 'numaym' an honoured kin to the Státimc Nation.

The dancing stops. Hunting Bear stands and holds his arms up. There is silence. His speech begins. This is his Potlatch, his gift giving feast, his chance to show how great a chief he is. The speech is long. There are many gifts to bestow. He welcomes elders from other tribes, moving slowly around the circle with presents; blankets, fishing tackle, a rifle, copper amulets and other treasures. Hunting Bear has a special gift for his newborn grandson. 'You have large feet,' he says. 'You will be called Sure Foot.' His youngest daughter and her partner, who are about to be married, receive a ski-doo.

I'm told to stand. Hunting Bear is pointing at me. 'A time ago, this white man emailed me with a question. Did I know of Jacob Cooper? I told him yes, I knew of Jacob Cooper. The elders of our tribe have kept his memory and the memory of Skaiya'm, his wife. He was a good man, an honest man. He treated us fairly and was a friend of the Státimc Nation. Our fathers welcomed him into the circle.

'The elders tell us Jacob and Skaiya'm had three children, Jack, Mary and Peter. Peter died as a young man, Jack became rich and left us leaving just Mary. We called her Dancing Raven. Dancing Raven is my family's ancestor, a grandmother of the Státimc Nation.' He paused and smiled.

'Welcome friend. I have two gifts for you. I make you a 'numaym' and to give you your Státimc name. You will be my little brother and your name will be Little Bear.'

Much has changed in the last year. A year ago when my father died, I discovered an old leather suitcase of his. Inside were fragile papers, a receipt for bullion made out to Jack Cooper issued by Hambros Bank in Toronto, a first class dinner menu from the SS Hiberna dated 1868 and a faded  photograph of a man. He wore a bowler hat and a suit with a Prince Albert hanging from his waistcoat pocket. It looked like a photographer's studio portrait taken with a painting of mountains as a backdrop. The sitter looked stiff and self-conscious as if he didn't want to be there. A name was scribbled on the back of the photograph in faint pencil, 'J.E. Cooper Esq.' That was the beginning of my search.

Today I have a new family, a big brother, sisters, nieces and a past I knew nothing of. My Státimc family call me Little Bear. You would have known me as John Cooper.

## Ode To Elodie
### By David Thorpe

**Prelude**

An ode is a poem praising or glorifying an event or individual containing three elements:

1. Strophe
2. Antistrophe
3. Epode.

'Rhetoric is the counterpart [literally, the antistrophe] of dialectic.' (Aristotle) Rhetorical methods are required in practical matters such as adjudicating a prudent course of action to be taken. Dialectical methods are necessary to find truth in theoretical matters.

A dialectical argument requires:

1. Thesis
2. Antithesis
3. Synthesis.

## 1. Strophe/Thesis

There was something odd about the Christmas tree. Now Jeffrey came to examine it, it wasn't a tree but an elder branch painted white jammed in a plant pot from which a few baubles randomly dangled. Tinsel hung disconsolately from the twigs.

He knew whose arty-farty idea that was. He accepted the glass of sherry from his son and sat on the only chair on which nothing had been abandoned. 'How's Elodie?'

'Fine.' His son, Simon, swigged at his G&T. 'Well, you know, if you take into account the–' he mouthed the words, '–time of the month. You alright?'

Jeffrey nodded. 'Fine, if you take into account the time of the century.'

'I'll go and see where everyone is.'

As he left, Jeffrey glanced at Elodie's father, Brian, who was asleep with his mouth open in the most comfortable chair.

Two minutes later an explosion of noise accompanied Simon and Elodie's three children as they tumbled over the sofa, sprawled on the floor, and skidded to a halt in front of the branch. Elodie glided in with a plate of mince pies and offered one to Jeffrey with a sweet smile. She was followed by Janet who sank, sighing, into a chair, jumping up immediately to remove a small Lego car.

Juniper, Holly and Acorn were furiously inspecting the labels on the gaudy parcels beneath the branch.

'That's mine! And that one!'

'Not fair! You've got the biggest!'

'I've got more.'

'Everyone got a drink?' asked Simon. Jeffrey noticed his glass was fuller than when he left the room.

'Shut up you lot!' yelled Elodie, and for a minute the kids were startled into silence.

A splutter from the comfiest chair. 'What? What?' Brian slammed his hands on its arms, eyes wide like golf balls.

'Never mind, Dad. We're going to open the presents.'

He relaxed. 'At last! I thought that'd never happen. We always used to do it in the mornings when you were growing up.'

'Well we do it in the afternoon in this house, when everyone's here,' Elodie told him. 'It's nicer that way. Everyone can see what everyone has given them and say thank you. Isn't it nicer, Simon?'

'Yes, of course, darling.'

'Can I go first?' yelled Juniper.

'No, me!' shouted Acorn.

'I want to!' squeaked Holly.

'We'll take it in turns, one present each, from the youngest to the oldest,' said Simon. 'That's fair.'

'Hurray!' cried Holly.

'Hmph. Last as usual.' Brian closed his eyes again.

While Juniper over-helped Holly to unwrap her present, doing most of it because she was so slow with the Sellotape, Elodie leaned over to Jeffrey. 'Sorry to hear about Caroline.'

Jeffrey kept his lips tight.

'You were too good for her. Don't you think you should look for someone more your own age?'

Jeffrey gripped the brandy glass so hard a mini-waterspout formed in the centre of the golden liquid. Before he could muster a response she had leapt to the branch, taking her tight smile with her, to yank Acorn from Juniper.

'I said one at a time!'

'Not quite so rough, sweetheart!' said Simon.

Juniper yelled at the top of his voice. 'What the hell is this?'

'Language!' said Janet. 'Where does he get it from!'

Juniper was waving a pair of socks like they smelt of dead fish. 'Socks! Socks! I asked for a RayBlast Monster! Everyone at school is getting one.'

'Patience darling. Who knows what's in your other presents?'

'It'd better be.' He threw the present down with a grimace and folded his arms.

'Be grateful for what you get, whatever it is.' Janet wagged a finger at him. 'That's how I was brought up. Honestly.'

'My turn now.' Elodie, eyes like Christmas lights, the red ones, picked up a silver-wrapped shape with a fake bow on the top. 'Who's this from? Ah, Mum!'

She tore the paper.

'If you undo it gently you can save the wrapping for next year,' said Janet.

Elodie fished out some printed fabric. 'Lovely,' she said as an apron fell loose to reveal the slogan 'Galley Slave' curled around a large, sweating woman surrounded by steam and piles of pans and dishes. 'Thank you so much, Mum.'

'Funny, isn't it? I saw you didn't have one, so...'

'No.' She folded it away. 'There might be a reason for that...'

'Your turn, Dad!' cried Acorn.

'Oh yes. Which one shall I open first?'

'Mine!' He thrust a small package at Simon.

'Right.' He ripped it open. 'Ah. Very thoughtful, Acorn. Thank you.' He put the hairbrush and comb set on the arm of his chair and smoothed his bald head with his other hand.

'Hadn't you noticed your father has no hair?' asked Janet.

'I forgot,' said Acorn.

Jeffrey saw no one else was doing it so he started tidying all the torn paper and gift tags into a plastic sack.

'I'm going to open this one.' Janet huffed as she eased her bulk onto the floor and stretched a Michelin Man arm out to grab the one from Simon and Elodie.

'What do you get for the woman who has everything?' said Simon.

Janet glared at him. 'That's not funny. Cor, it's heavy.' She tore off the wrapping which Jeffrey grabbed immediately. 'Hold your horses,' she told him. Her face fell. 'A kilo of dog food.' She let the plastic sack fall on the floor.

'Expensive dog food,' said Simon.

'The best,' said Elodie. 'We know how much you love Poopsie.'

'Who is right now pining in the kennels because you wouldn't let us bring him.' Janet glared down her nose.

'Last year he slobbered all over Holly and totally freaked her out then peed on the new carpet,' said Simon.

'It's his way of showing affection,' said Janet.

'Well this is so he doesn't feel left out,' said Elodie.

Janet shoved it under the sofa.

'Me next,' said Jeffrey. 'I'll open this one, from you two. At least I don't have a dog.' Jeffrey took a book-shaped package from the floor. 'It's a book.'

'Brilliant, Dad,' said Simon.

'Great. I wonder what it is? A racy thriller, perhaps, or a Booker-prize-winner. You know I like a good novel.' The wrapper was thrust into the plastic sack before he even glanced at the front cover. Then he read: "The Great Mate Guide: How to Achieve Long-Lasting Success in a Relationship'. What the–'

'We thought it would be useful,' said Elodie.

'Based on your experiences,' said Simon.

'It's very good,' said Elodie.

'We just want you to be happy,' said Simon.

'Ah, that's nice,' said Janet. 'Isn't that nice, Brian? They want Jeffrey to be happy.'

Brian snored.

'It's – it's –' With an effort, Jeffrey remembered it was Christmas. 'It's – very kind of you.' He opened it at random and read: 'Mates are usually chosen based on the characteristics of a person's parents – both good and bad – and relationships typically fail because the bad characteristics are not fully recognised and challenged'. He looked at his son and wondered what characteristics of his mother, who right now was living in the South of France with a B-list fashion mogul, Simon saw in Elodie. Avarice? Slovenliness? They certainly weren't his own mother's.

'Grandpa!' yelled all the kids at once, jumping on Brian's generous stomach as if he was a floor cushion. 'Your turn!'

'Agh! What the bloody hell–?' Brian's mouth and golf-ball eyes pinged open again, his arms and legs shot out, his left arm knocking Acorn sideways and his right arm dislodging a vase from the window-sill.

'It's your turn, Dad,' said Elodie. 'Come on, wake up, pay attention. Honestly. You don't deserve any presents.'

'That's no way to talk to your father,' said Janet.

'Well what's the point of coming here if he's going to spend the whole time comatose?' Elodie threw back her G&T.

'I don't want a bloody present!' he snuffled. 'Not if I'm going to be insulted.'

'Here. Open this.' Simon threw a small parcel at his belly and it bounced off. The kids laughed. He managed to catch it and his arthritic fingers fumbled with the tape. Everyone calmed down during the five minutes it took him to get it off except Juniper who chewed Acorn's hair until he hit him.

'Hope it's not something for the dog,' said Janet.

It was a rubber bone.

'Thank you very much. I don't know why I bothered to wake up.' Jeffrey reached for the wrapping paper but Brian snatched it away. 'Get off! At least let me keep this!' He closed his eyes, smoothed out the creases, placed it over his face, and lay back.

'Grandpa's funny!' said Holly. 'My turn again!' Snatching the nearest package she ripped it apart. 'A joke book!' She opened it up and read, slowly, "What thinks roads are both dangerous and a source of food?"

'Dad!' yelled Juniper, which made everyone except Simon laugh.

'Why me?' he asked.

'Remember when you insisted on cooking a dead pheasant we found on the road and were throwing up for four days?' said Elodie.

'You're wrong!' shouted Holly. 'It's birds.'

'Oh my God! The turkey!' cried Elodie and rushed to the kitchen.

'Uh-oh,' said Acorn. 'Mum's burnt the Christmas dinner again.'

'Tut. I did invite you to our house for Christmas,' said Janet. 'You'd never get burnt dinner there. It would be perfect. All the trimmings. Cranberry jelly. Bacon.'

'Mmm, bacon,' was heard from beneath the wrapping paper.

'Proper stuffing, not from a packet.'

'Aye, I spend all year dreaming of that. Then we come here,' spake the wrapping paper once more.

'Thank you, Brian,' said Simon. 'I'll have you know Elodie's been planning this for weeks. I'm sure it will be fine. I'll go and see if she needs a hand.'

'But what about opening the presents?' wailed Acorn. 'It's my turn next.'

'Wait till we get back–' Simon left.

'Oh...' Acorn stuck out his lower lip.

To distract him, Jeffrey asked, 'So Acorn, what are you doing at school these days?'

Acorn burst into tears.

In the kitchen, Elodie was poking at a charred corpse. 'Look! Look at it! And I followed the instructions!'

Simon leapt to the blistered bird and started peeling the black skin off. 'It's alright...'

'It's ruined! Oh, what will mother say? I knew this would happen. It's her fault.'

'Calm down. It's just a little carbonara; people like that these days.'

'They'll crucify me!' She picked up a knife and pointed it at Simon. 'Wait. This is your fault.'

He backed away. 'What–? Why?'

She advanced on him, waving the knife. 'You chose the cooker. It's clearly wrong. I put it in for two hours at one hundred and sixty as the recipe said and look at it! It can't be calibrated correctly. It's too hot.'

Simon put his hands up. 'Honey. Put the knife down. Please. Then we can talk.'

'I won't put the knife down till you fix the dinner.'

Simon was backed up to the kitchen counter and could go no further. 'Sweetheart, I love you.'

'Liar.'

'Remember the time of month.'

She thrust the knife point up to his throat. 'That's got nothing to do with it!' she yelled. 'I feel... myself. Like when I was thirteen–'

'An adolescent–'

'–And everything was crystal clear and I realised I'd been hoodwinked by my parents all my childhood into thinking they were right and I had to do everything they said. Everything made sense. The good, the bad, and the–'

'–ambiguous and unexplained,' Simon inched sideways.

'I no longer feel like I'm supposed to be 'womanly' and 'nice to everyone' and 'smooth over the cracks', because that's what 'good women' are supposed to do while men can do what they like. Why should I fulfil the patriarchy's expectations?'

'You're totally right,' said Simon.

'You're just saying that!' cried Elodie.

'No, I mean it. Your mum is an unreasonable cow. My dad manages to be a perfectionist and a failure. Your dad is a lazy complainer who hates everyone. I am lousy at roadkill, and our kids are ungrateful wretches. Except Holly.'

'Only because she hasn't learnt how to be yet.'

Elodie put the knife down. Simon draped his arm around her and she rested her head on his shoulder.

Janet and Jeffrey waltzed into the kitchen. Their eyes switched between them and the burnt bird. No one spoke for a full minute.

Janet set to work expertly slicing the turkey. 'This is fine. This bit's alright. So's this. It's very juicy, really. Not at all dry...'

Jeffrey fished out the roast potatoes and stuffing. 'Hey! Real stuffing! Excellent. I'll just put these veg on to boil and it'll be ready real soon.'

'There's the cranberry jelly!' Janet said. 'You have some!'

'And the white sauce!' Simon showed her a jug.

'You've prepared everything after all.' Janet placed the pile of turkey slices and wings under a sheet of foil. 'I'll keep these warm under the grill.'

Simon stroked his wife's hair. 'There we are.' He smiled at her. 'Everything's sorted. It's going to be a fantastic meal. We can finish opening the presents after we've eaten.' He looked around. 'Anyone for another drink?'

Elodie nodded. 'Cup of tea, please.'

## 2. Antistrophe/Antithesis

After an appropriate amount of time – sufficient not to seem impolitely hasty to anyone – Elodie uttered a plausible reason for going upstairs. The bathroom mirror reflected a face which she barely recognised: drawn by forces over which she had no control or knowledge into a caricature of the face she had once known, as if a trickster god had tweaked the clay from which it was made in amounts guaranteed to confirm her worst suspicions about what lay beneath the surface, and the secret habits which had led to them. The gray eyes were never hers; they had been her mother's mother's. Nor did she recognise the right to be there of the broken veins on the insides of the oversized nostrils, that had a tendency to flare along with her unpredictable outbursts, that shamed her, having a life independent of her conscious will.

She took from her handbag the small strip of plastic with the red line on it and stared at it.

This face within the mirror over the washbasin, and the body to which it was attached which could never be completely seen no matter how far forward she leaned, inhabited an enviable universe into which she never allowed a single other human being. For she always locked the door when she came alone into the bathroom; it was the only time in her life that she could be confident of solitude.

With this confidence she could lose the sensation – otherwise always with her – of an omnipresent observer to her rear, sometimes male, sometimes female, always critical. That universe beyond the glass was hers alone; into it she would step to experience its glorious privacy. And this is what she did now. Downstairs – from where shrieks of emotion carried through the joists and tiles – was another world to which she did not feel she belonged. When she was within it she felt she was merely playing a part that had been written for her, in a genre that was not to her liking, for an unseen audience whose laughter at her foolishness could not be heard, but of which she was acutely aware; and there was nothing to be done about it. The script she and her family members had been assigned ran along grooves predetermined by further forces of which she could not know. She doubted that they were the province of the same trickster god as distorted her own face, suspecting instead that it was directed by customs and constrictions laid down in distant boardrooms by over-self-indulgent executives who themselves played parts written by others – and so on ad infinitum. The universe into which she had stepped was written into no scripts; there, she was able to reach a level of calmness unknowable in the former universe, as she observed its behaviours and saw with a clarity beyond telescopic how the parts being played by the individuals to whom she was bound on her journey through life were as those of couriers, who were transporting ever onward – through the cascading rhythms of time – transgenerational passengers in the form of: biota or biomes comprising hundreds of thousands of members of species of archaea, enzymes and bacteria; of learned and transmitted behaviour patterns and social expectations; of odd associations of words and phrases, and accreted genetic predispositions and qualities. Of most of these they were blissfully unaware. Were she able to transport herself backwards or forwards in time, to witness her ancestors or descendants acting in concert as they were today, she would no doubt recognise these self-similar affectations, lifescripts, miens, mannerisms and attitudes; and thereby be forced to acknowledge her own lack of individuation. The process which had manufactured Elodie was an aleatory randomising of a limited palette of ingredients spiced by the occasional exotic input.

As messengers little better than carrier pigeons operating within a bubble of curtailed cognisance, with truncated abilities to affect their environment, choices or life directions, she could perceive from within this other universe the gravitational paths which her family members followed; just as the planet to which they were tied looped both around the Sun and simultaneously around the centre of the spiral galaxy – in one of whose arms she had been told by books and teachers it had its home – but the length of its orbit in terms of millions or tens of millions of years she did not know. Illimitable periodicities within periodicities in a non-linear cyclical temporality. Like her galaxy – one of many billions she was given to believe were hurtling constantly away from each other at unimaginable speeds – at the heart of her brain was a black hole that consumed her. As the huge and fearsome Sun is filled with burning hydrogen gas, Elodie was filled with incandescent shame at the colossal vastness of her own lack of consciousness and stupidity but at least, she told herself, I am aware of this much. I can intuit the existence of just the tiniest corner of this phenomenology; even if the only clue she could leave herself and her family in that universe over there (that living room below) was her pathetic attempt to assert some level of individual expression of differentiation by replacing the traditional Christmas tree with a painted branch of elder, that tree so revered by pagans before the arrival of invaders to British shores, along with the holly and oak and yew. But even that was not original.

Comets would one day enter the solar system of this family and a few would be captured by its gravity to be pinned forevermore within its bounds, but not until Holly and Juniper and Acorn were of an age to bond with a mate. They would only be recognised as potential co-parenting material because of similar habituated traits to their own and herself and Simon, and their parents, and so on; for this was the lure of the familiar – whether beneficial or not – and the need for completion; whether satisfied in childhood or not. Thoughts of whether this was a cause for celebration or despair repeatedly tortured Elodie. They were most severe at times of hormonal stress. This seemed to peel away a skin from the world, to reveal something of its hidden motives, and to lend her momentary feelings of alienation and otherness that derive from possessing overmuch clear-sightedness.

She had considered religion. There could be no God worth investing her faith in to which she felt able to expose her vulnerability, who could sanction (as happened all the time) not just the destruction of a city caused by an erupting volcano, or even of a solar system caused by a nova event, both of which were trivial beside the collision of two galaxies and the consequent destruction of all uncountable and unknowable lives therein – unless this level of death was at the service of an even higher purpose. But what could it be? From families of minute archaea, to families of larger fauna such as humans, to solar families of planets and galactic – even pan-galactic – families of stars and stardust ever dying and eternally being reborn within and at the service of the perpetuation of the cosmic laws and habits that determined them; all were both trapped and sustained by them. And this was the recognition bestowed upon her by the perspective gained from situating her consciousness in the mirror universe – with all the munificence of the most tragi-comic yet desirable seasonal gift.

Bearing this gift within her carefully, she stepped back into the populated universe; washed the hands that were connected to her face; flushed the toilet to remove the plastic strip she had thrown into it; took one last glance in the mirror to check both its permanence and the state of her hair; and left the room.

## 3. Epode/Thesis

Around the dinner table, with its central decoration of greenery collaring a red wax candle and which was edged with eight set places – each given a cracker containing a bad joke and a paper hat, sat the other members of her immediate family. They smiled at her with forgiving smiles, kind smiles, smiles tinged with impatience and expectation of the meal to follow imminently.

'Alright, darling?' Simon eased her chair in for her.

'Yes thank you. I'm sorry I kept you all waiting.'

Unfolding her napkin she knew how the conversation would flow, beginning with the denials of a need for an apology. And she knew she should be as grateful as they for the security of the familiarity of the repetition of this annual ritual. So she participated in the chinking of wine glasses, snapped the crackers open, read in turn the bad joke she found within hers, placed the stupid hat on her head, and distributed the Brussels sprouts. Passing the cranberry jelly, she settled into her role, spoke her lines – for it was effortful to do otherwise and she was tired. Pouring her gravy, she thought perhaps that she did not give the others enough credit, and that they, too, consciously acted their parts selflessly for the sake of the family cohesion. Chewing her turkey, she wondered, if so, what they would be like, were they not to do so.

With this is mind, she gazed at her father and mother and father-in-law – while spearing roast potatoes – and sought to look beyond their expressions at their true faces, that they themselves might see in their own bathroom mirrors. But this was a pointless game; because she had also played it many times before, at other family events, each year of her conscious life, and emerged none the wiser. It was a habit as ingrained and learned as pulling the crackers. As a hormonal teenager, she had attempted to force the true faces to appear, with what she believed to be penetrating questions or shocking behaviour; but to no avail. The inertia of normality was too great for her puniness; and indeed her own abnormality was part of the greater normality. This was the acutely-felt irony of her predetermined role.

As she viewed her husband and father-in-law side-by-side, with their identical habits of chewing with their mouths open, she ran through the number ways of ways in which this could end. For she did not think it that she could endure another year of this, another Christmas like this at the end of it. But then she had felt the same last Christmas – and the one before. The procession of generations, of which she was already an indelible part repeating the same uninspired and dispiriting conversations, could not be allowed to perpetuate. Separating – with a dull weight in her heart once more – the bickering Juniper from Acorn, brought home that it was already too late to remove her responsibility for the continuation of this process. Divorce would achieve nothing, nor would removing herself to the far side of the world; they were the wrong solutions to the wrong problem; the damage was already done, and would continue to be done.

Her question, 'Why don't we all go for walk?' was met with the kids protesting 'But it's getting dark outside,' and 'But we want to play video games,' and stupefied silence from the adults; so she didn't add 'It will make a nice change'. A change would signify something. But even if there was a change, it would still be impossible to escape the all-encompassing perpetuity of this gyre, short of parricide, infanticide and suicide. No medical procedure could banish her microscopic symbiotic passengers; only a lengthy and prohibitively expensive course of counselling would correct the ingrained herited ripostes of a lifetime. For her solitary effort was wanting.

After too much pudding with brandy sauce, and with the dishes cleared away and everyone seated back in the living room, she blocked their view of the screen, zeroed the volume, and to the seven puzzled faces admitted: 'I want to apologise to you all. Again. I'm sorry. The thing is, I made a mistake about the reason why my hormones are a bit up-and-down.' She swallowed. She regarded Simon cuddling Holly, and Acorn with his arm around Juniper, quiet for once, and her parents in symmetrical chairs, and Jeffrey steepling his fingers, and continued, 'I'm not menstrual. I'm going to have another baby.'

The faces creased, and she finally could not withhold her own tears.

# Too Young To Be Old
### By John Thompson

'The problem with a man is that although his body may be sixty, his mind still thinks that it is sixteen.' He was unable to recall who had said that - some guru or yogi he had come across in his youthful travels in India, he guessed - but the fact was that they had come back to haunt him. Here he was, rapidly approaching his sixtieth birthday, and life had slapped him in the face.

Desmond Twogood was a handsome man; had been all his life. He had been the bonniest baby, the most captivating youth, the most dashingly good-looking young man, and even now, in what he had hitherto regarded merely as late middle-age, his face was still remarkably handsome.

He had very early in life come to appreciate that his face was his fortune, and had accordingly taken very good care of himself. Even though he now had a few wrinkles to show for the life of debauchery into which his good looks and lascivious inclinations had led him, he was able to disguise them quite effectively. He made full use of all the anti-ageing creams and unguents that were aimed, he assumed, primarily at the female market, and he also took regular exercise to ensure that any excesses of food and drink - and there had been plenty - were controlled, allowing him to boast a lean and relatively muscular physique. Hair colouring helped to disguise his age, though lately he had permitted a touch of grey to remain at the temples, to give himself a distinguished appearance.

It has to be admitted that Desmond had failed abysmally to live up to his name, having been very far from good - let alone too good! Women had fluttered about him like butterflies around a buddleia bush, and he had married and divorced four of them, all possessed of substantial means, and profited accordingly. He had almost always gained something, in addition to the obvious sexual advantages, from every woman he had ever had a relationship with, however brief. Hard as it may seem for the average man to understand, women simply enjoyed giving Desmond presents, even though he was without doubt the sort of man who could best be described as - to use a somewhat old-fashioned, but in Desmond's case entirely appropriate, term - a cad.

And let us not be under any misapprehension. Desmond was by no means a mere gigolo, using his physical charms to ensnare rich old ladies willing to pay for his company. Though by no means averse to a relationship with an older woman, as long as she remained attractive (and, of course, well-heeled), his conquests invariably tended to be younger than himself. At the age of forty-three he had married the twenty-something heiress to a fortune, a brief but lucrative liaison. Even in his fifties Desmond was still casting his eyes upon females considerably younger than himself, often with a degree of success that eluded men twenty years his junior.

But now his carefully constructed world had come crashing down: his ego had been shattered, his confidence drained. He had not left his flat for a fortnight, nor exercised or even shaved during that time. When he accidentally caught a glimpse of himself in a mirror, he had seemingly aged decades in no more than a few days, horribly like the portrait of Dorian Gray. Wrinkles had appeared like magic and his eyes, now sunken, had lost their lustre. And all because of one silly little tart!

He had been sauntering down the High Street to collect his newspaper, and indulge in a cappuccino at Luigis, when his eye had been caught by a girl walking on the other side of the road. She was quite simply the most beautiful creature he had ever set eyes upon, which was saying a lot. Her face was a perfect oval, her eyes large and almond-shaped, her nose exquisitely elegant, her pouting lips so delectably kissable, her figure quite perfect, her legs sublimely shapely, and her entire poise one of extreme elegance.

Desmond had stopped to look at her, quite overcome by her loveliness, and then, to his surprise (and gratification, it must be said), she too had stopped. She regarded him for a second, then began to cross the street, threading her way elegantly through the early morning traffic. As she drew near she smiled with the smile of a veritable angel, and then addressed him.

'Wasser matter, grandad? Need an 'and across the road?

# Homecoming
## By David Thorpe

I was struggling to picture Anna's legs: long, slender, smooth. Intending to evoke desire, instead I found gratitude: that she was my wife, and desirable, pretty, smart; and for the fact that multiple images of her were available in my memory bank to call upon as needed. Like now...

...As I knelt behind my 89-year old mother, unclothed but for bandages wound tight round her swollen limbs, from feet to thighs, clutching a towel so old that I had forgotten the first time I saw it. There was a job to do.

–Make sure I'm dry, she said. –I can't reach round there.

There were many things she couldn't do and this was the most intimate. It would be necessary to insinuate between the folds and within the cracks of senescent flesh. Her wrinkled backside brought to mind two giant puffballs squashed together, matured to the point when the slightest touch would trigger an explosion of black seedsmoke. I dismissed this, another irreverent image. I worked as gently as I could, patting the fragile skin dry.

I stayed safely where I was. Above me hung oil paintings of tempestuous waves exploding on granite slabs made by my father out of respect for my mother's passion for the sea that, ever since his death fourteen years previously, had been on her bedroom wall. I had no enthusiasm to move to the front. I was decidedly averse to the view that would ensue. Certain images would fix themselves in my memory bank, that can't be washed over like a painting, to lurk there like time-bombs ready to ambush me at inappropriate moments: such as when comfortably between Anna's legs – popping up like a sick prank – of empty drooping paps, the final mortality of it, and I'd lose it, no going back, shrunk to one fifth the man I had been moments earlier, Anna staring at me in confusion, disappointment.

So I performed my task with as little visual engagement as necessary.

But then there was the odour; it emanated from between the fleshy folds. Smell may not be ignored, a fact all the more true if it be repulsive. Her horrible arthritis and sad inability to balance rendered her unable to clean herself; she couldn't shower because of the bandages. Anyway, she was afraid of falling in the shower (although I'd bought a folding stool small enough to fit within it). Detritus lay fast, encrusted within.

Poor woman. Was she even aware of this? I knew what I ought to do, and if I loved her I would. What was the problem? It was the kind of thing carers and nurses did twenty times a day: take a flannel, soap it, wriggle around in those most private of places where I imagined only one man had ever been.

But this was my mother, and I would have to penetrate right between her legs.

My mother, a keen tennis player from her own childhood, had taught me the game. On grass and on peach-coloured hard courts she had patiently coaxed better serves and back-handers from my awkward arms. Once, she won the All-Yorkshire Women's Doubles. She had encouraged me to cycle, too, beginning by transporting me as a toddler in a wicker basket on the front of her heavy Dutch-style bicycle. After I had graduated via stabilisers to a child's Raleigh we would set off from home and pedal up the hill through two miles of council estate to the nearest countryside, to picnic in the old village churchyard on sandwiches and cake. These were just some of the achievements recorded on the curriculum vitae of her lower limbs.

After I had been separated from my mother, eased out (with cold, cruel forceps) from between those limbs, longer ago than either of us cared to consider, we had been immediately separated. I was six weeks premature and, on account of my mother not being well and I being sickly, the nurses removed me to an upstairs room. We were kept apart for my first three weeks of life.

When we were reunited not much changed. She confessed to me when I was in my forties that she had taken as scientifically established the advice she had read in a 1950s childcare manual that too much cuddling and hugging spoiled a child. Though love was a current that could pass between us, it was not to be conducted through our capable arms, into our practical hands, via our tentative fingertips. She expressed her love (partly) with her other pair of limbs.

So I delved with a flannel, my eyes as averted as was practicable, rummaging blindly for the source of the fetor, replacing malodour with the fragrance of Cussons Imperial Leather. What was passing through her mind as I ferreted about in her nether regions? Was she as unnerved as I? Outwardly she endured it in silence. I remembered with sadness the slenderness of her ankles as I observed how elephantine they now were. They must have attracted my father once.

I emptied the bowl down the toilet. I supported her over the snail-paced two metres back to the bed, braced her while she manoeuvred into her approach path and dropped into a seated position. Following exact instructions I fetched a bra and a pair of large white knickers. I helped her into them –

– while conjuring Anna, in a black lacy set of bra and knickers I had bought her, scented with her lotion of choice: orange and bergamot. Against her pale, smooth skin, the delicate embroidery never failed to excite. But after a few seconds, as I was hooking the bra behind my mother's back, pulling the elastic tight against her flaccid skin, I was stricken by the thought that by confounding the two images in my mind – the one I wished to efface, and the one I wished to recall – I risked cementing a link that might invert counterproductively at some future inopportune moment.

In desperation I began scrabbling in the memory bank for alternative deposited impressions. Gave up. Observed the sadness in my mum's face; hugged her.

–Is that better? I asked. –Is that alright?

Two days' earlier. Boxing Day. Anna and I had driven 220 miles from our home to my mother's house, arriving in the middle of the afternoon as the sky was darkening. We let ourselves in to find my mother dozing in her chair in the gloomy back room. She had been sleeping there every night for two weeks. She had not changed her clothes.

–I'm frightened to go upstairs, she said. –I might fall.

She'd had a fall on the twelfth of December. We already knew that. Younger people, whose legs work correctly, fall. Older people have a fall.

–I didn't break anything, she said. –I was lucky. I don't know how I did it. One minute I was standing up. The next–

We dropped the bags of Christmas presents and rushed forward. Anna knelt in front of her and raised her skirt. Both legs were at least twice their normal size, the shiny skin stretched like balloons about to burst. Her right leg was as white as chalk except where the skin was plum with bruises and raw with sores. A bandage concealed her calf.

–I can feel water seeping down my leg, she said. –But I don't think I've had an accident.

Anna touched it and flinched. –It's stone cold and sopping wet.

Gangrene was perhaps an hour or two off. If it took hold, hospital would be inevitable, a sentence my mother dreaded more than any other. If the gangrene didn't end her life, the ordeal of the ward regime would.

I said: –You've been sitting here for two weeks and not had your legs up. Surely you know better?

She had known in the past. She'd done it before. While I called NHS Direct, Anna lifted her legs onto a stool and removed the saturated bandage. Gently, she rubbed the leg to revive the circulation. Within an hour a healthier pinkness had returned to the skin. A doctor arrived after five hours. He stayed fifteen minutes and sent for a district nurse, who came around midnight and applied dressings as large as plaster casts. They both threaded into the house a sense that we were a single stitch in a day spent darning lives that had come undone at the seams. Miscellaneous victims of seasonal misfortune: lonely old people suffering from winter flu or domestic accidents, freezing people stranded penniless in draughty homes, careless people who had over-celebrated and had accidents or got into a brawl, frightened people whose husbands had attacked them, children fighting pneumonia.

On the 27th Anna took the car away. Her own family commitments beckoned. I was marooned.

While I was easing mum into her dress, it dawned on me that Anna had saved her life.

–I don't know what's going to happen to me, she said suddenly. – I want to die.

–But I don't want you to die, I said. –Some joy would leave the world with you. Please don't think like that, Mum.

None of her pairs of shoes could fit over her bulbous, bandaged feet, so I trimmed the tops off a pair of thick pink woollen socks and gently eased them over her heels. Finally, before me was a woman of some charm, in a dress of a blue that matched her eyes, trimmed with Nottingham lace, accessorised with a delicate pink cardigan, pearl earrings and a coral necklace. Subtle make-up had been applied – lipstick and a dash of powder. You might be forgiven for thinking she was twenty years younger from the waist up. I kissed her.

I helped her to the landing and onto the stairlift. I stood there and watched her glide down, waving like a queen on a grand yacht being seen off by crowds on the wharfside. She disappeared from view round the corner, the yacht cruising round the headland for the calm open waters. I gazed at the wall now revealed, where there hung an arrangement of my father's miniature watercolours of birds: chaffinch, robin, great tit and lark. I could almost hear a new dawn chorus.

Two days later, having choreographed a battery of carers, nurses and visitors who would arrive in succession during the day to dress, wash and cook for her, change her dressings and clean the house, I took the train home. That night I lay between Anna's legs, re-entered our world and cordoned off the rest.

–Thank you, I whispered in her ear.

# A Chance Encounter

By Maya Sales-Hyde

As Edward Smith climbed the stairs to the rooftop he thought again with bemusement that it was a shame he hadn't worn his pinstripe suit. The outfit had sat in the back of his wardrobe for the past 16 years unworn, and it seemed that if there had ever been an occasion for him to wear a garish suit then this was it.

For New Year's Eve it was surprisingly quiet, the only sound being the tired thud of his footsteps against the floor. Somewhere in the building below him a door slammed, then opened and shut again. Edward had wanted his ascent to be pensively dramatic, but this was hindered by the fact that every five minutes or so he had to stop and catch his breath. After spending the majority of his late 40s sitting down, this amount of strenuous activity was extremely shocking.

*Maybe I should go through what I intend to say,* he said to himself as the last flight of stairs came into sight. *Of course no one will listen to it, but it seems as though something ought to be said to mark the event.*

Edward had never been eccentric or interesting enough to have many little quirks, but the one thing that he had fanatically believed in throughout his life was whole numbers. He would wake up at exactly 7:00 every morning, and go to bed at exactly 22:00 every night. Instead of buying loaves of bread he would always buy rolls, ensuring that he was never faced with the dilemma of whether or not to leave one half eaten. If ever he read a book that was part of a series, regardless of his opinion on it (which was often very disagreeable), he would read all the others with a stoic fanaticism.

It was due to this that he had waited until New Years Eve to jump off the top of his apartment building, because it seemed that after a lifetime of striving for whole numbers, ending his life half-way through the year would be a bit of a cop out.

Upon opening the door that led into the small, untidy rooftop, where generations of tenants had tried and failed to grow various plants in a number of chipped terracotta pots, Edward stopped short. To his great surprise there was already someone standing in the exact same spot that he had been planning on being for the past 4 months and 13 days. Completely unsure what the protocol was in situations like this, Edward lingered by the door, his plump face turning even pinker with indignation.

*Just my luck,* he huffed, nervously tapping his fingers together. *Somebody beat me to it.*

A part of him was quite tempted to call out to the person that they had jolly well better get down because they had most likely not been thinking about this moment for the past 4 months and 13 days, and in his most humble opinion this took precedence over whatever whim they were following. But then of course if it was a whim, he would rather not startle them and have them fall to a death that had not been meticulously prepared for, as that seemed a bit of a waste.

Before Edward had to think any further, the figure let out a howl and stumbled backwards into a heap on the floor. The sniffling made up his mind for him, and he warily approached the body. He coughed apprehensively. The bundle didn't seem to notice, and carried on wailing with enough force that Edward would hardly have been shocked if one of the plant pots had shattered there and then. He coughed again, louder this time. Still no reaction.

Feeling that this was getting him nowhere, and still suffering from the indignation of the situation, Edward leant down and firmly shook what he assumed was the person's shoulder. A louder shriek was emitted and he discovered a little too late that the 'shoulder' was in fact a knee, that had just made contact with his shin. At this point Edward had quite lost his patience. Grabbing hold of the person he said with as much force as he could muster,

'For goodness sake stop this racket at once. Some of us would like to conduct our final moments with a little more solemnity.'

The figure slowly rose into a sitting position, and Edward finally discovered that it was, in fact, a young girl of about 22, with curly red hair matted with tears and snot.

Her bloodshot eyes looked at him with a surprising amount of hostility as she croaked, 'Go find another roof arsehole. This one's taken.'

Edward could not believe his misfortune. After a lifetime of dissatisfaction, his final chance was being foiled.

'I most certainly will not. I have been planning this day for 4 months and 13 days, and I will not change those plans because of your operatic screeching.'

The girl didn't seem to have anything to say to this, and they sat in silence. Distant sounds of celebration could be heard over the dull whistling of the wind. A taunting reminder of the world they had removed themselves from.

'Why?' She asked quietly, tears still streaming down her face as she stared resolutely ahead, wrapping the threadbare sweater tighter around her.

'Pardon?'

'Why have you been planning this for 4 months and 15 days?'

'13 days.'

'Whatever.'

Edward wasn't exactly sure how to answer this. How could you explain to someone so young the gradual loss of anything resembling hope as your life slowly got duller and duller, until it couldn't quite be called living at all? The life changing chemotherapy that should have been a turning point, but didn't seem to effect any change. Wondering whether the weeks and months of suffering had been for nothing.

The girl was looking at him expectantly. *Ah well, perhaps this is my chance to make a final dramatic speech.*

He began tentatively, 'It wasn't as though my life stopped being worth living, it was that I realised that it had never been worth very much anyway.' He stopped, and glanced at her, but she seemed to be expecting him to continue, and Edward found with surprise that he wanted to. 'I've never been very good at anything you see. When I was growing up I didn't think that that mattered, and that one could live a perfectly happy, talentless life. But then I realised that this also meant I had nothing to strive for. I've had the same job for 30 years, and every day I hate it a little bit more. When you're young it seems as though the world is your stage, and that you are performing in a play that has no definite plot, but I know now exactly what will happen tomorrow, and the day after, and if you asked me I could give an extremely detailed itinerary of the second Tuesday of next July.

'I thought that perhaps if I met someone extraordinary, my life would stop being so ordinary. But no one incredible wants to commit themselves to boring mundanity. At least that's what I've found. I was with Agatha for two years, and when she ended it she told me that if she had to spend one more day with me, she would rip out all her hair.'

Edward trailed off, realising that he had never said any of this out loud before. Although he had thought about it plenty of times, it was an entirely different feeling to hear his own voice saying it. He shrugged helplessly, the sudden understanding of his situation bringing a feeling of heartrending misery.

'I had cancer you know.' His voice was feeble now, fighting against the lump forming in his throat. 'Of the colon. They said it was a miracle I made it through. When I got out of the hospital I wanted to celebrate by calling everyone I knew and telling them the good news. The only people in my life who cared about the outcome of my treatment were my landlady, who wanted to know if she could rent out my flat to someone else, and my boss, who wanted to know whether or not he needed to hire someone else. I quit my job. I thought that this was the moment that I would start living every day to the fullest, I would travel and see the world, meet extraordinary people, and maybe even become one myself. But you can't travel the world when you only have £300 in your bank account.

'So I asked for my job back, and I told myself that I would religiously save up, and that in exactly a year I would go off and see the world. That was three years ago, and somehow, despite the saving religiously, I still only have £300 in my bank account.'

'You know, meeting someone extraordinary isn't all it's cracked up to be,' the girl said in a defeated voice, 'In fact, sometimes it's the worst thing that can happen to you.'

Edward didn't agree with that statement in the slightest, but he waited for her to continue, extending her the same courtesy that she had given to him.

'I was at Cambridge Studying politics. I was going to become the next Caroline Lucas.'

Edward didn't know who this was, but thought it impolite to interrupt.

'Everyone always told me that I was destined for great things, and I believed them. Of course I did. Why shouldn't I? For some reason I expected everything to fall into my lap, because even though in theory I knew that the world was unfair, I never thought it would be for me.

'Then two things happened. One was amazing and one devastating, and they happened one after the other. First of all I met Him. I'd never loved anyone before. It felt like staring over the side of a boat in the middle of the ocean, and wondering what would happen if I jumped. And all of a sudden I was falling into deep water without any hope of resurfacing.

'A month afterwards my mum was hit by a lorry that had carried on going even after the lights turned amber. And it felt like the sun had stopped shining on the earth. He was all I had left, and I gave him everything. He was an artist, and he wanted to travel, like you. He wanted to see the Northern Lights and the Taj Mahal. I left Cambridge and I took out all the money I had, left the friends I had made and the future I had so carefully arranged. It took me until Iceland to realise that his heart was a wanderer too, and until Paris to understand that it would never stop being so.

'So now I have nothing and no one, and I can't blame anyone but my foolish self.'

Again they sat in silence, but it was far denser this time, neither of them knowing quite what to say, understanding that there were perhaps no words that would make the other feel any differently. Edward felt that it was very important that he find a way to convince her not to give up hope, but didn't know how to do so without doing the same thing himself. *She has her whole life ahead of her.* He thought to himself. *She is talented, and was once driven, all the things that a lack of has led me to where I am today. And yet here she is, intending to do the exact same thing that I am.*

'Why didn't you jump?' he asked, keeping his voice as gentle as possible. 'You say you have nothing, but if that was true surely you wouldn't have stopped yourself.'

She laughed bitterly but didn't reply, which Edward took as encouragement to continue.

'It seems to me that you have rather a lot. For one thing you clearly have potential and I am sure if you tried hard enough you could get back into Cambridge. Which would probably also fix your problem with money. I don't wish to seem impertinent, but it seems as though going through with what you intend to do would be a great waste of a life that still has everything to be decided.'

She shrugged, but the dishevelled jumper was no longer being held around her like armour. *How funny, that she has had everything that I have always wished for, but is no happier because of it.*

'There are things you could still do you know.' She remarked, unapologetically steering the conversation away from herself. 'You could take evening classes, learn something new. You could start online dating, people are always meeting on there. You just need the determination to make the change, even if it takes longer than you expect. Maybe you gave up too quickly the first time round, wanted everything to be miraculous straight away.'

*Determination.* That one word captured his interest. Perhaps in the end, talent had little to do with it. Without realising it, while considering this possibility, Edward Smith experienced his 14th sunrise after 4 months and 13 days of hoping he would never see one again.

# Someone To Hold
## By Peter Barker

At such times I feel a fleeting fear for my own sanity as I watch the clean-up team at work. I'm sat in my seat, staring through the windscreen, a man in a white suit is wiping the glass, smearing the blood. There are chunks of grey stuff that he has to pick off and I know what they are, so does he. I've seen it before but still I feel the urge to vomit.

I throw open the door and swing down onto the tracks. A light breeze wafts the putrid smell of guts around me and I turn to retch. Why do they do it? Don't they know what it's like for us? Do they care? Selfish bastards.

I stumble over the stones at the edge of the track as I skirt around the poor sods having to pick up the pieces. I was two minutes from the end of my shift, a mile from my change-over station and half an hour from home. I start walking.

'Hey Drive, where you going?' someone shouts behind me. I don't answer, it's taking all my concentration to keep my legs from folding under me. Someone else is going to have to get this one into the station, not me. I simply can't do this anymore.

I can breath now, I've walked twenty maybe thirty yards and the air is clear, clean, fresh. My head has stopped spinning. But something tugs at my mind, something is wrong. I want to talk to Josie, I want to fall into her arms, I want her to tell me it's all okay, but it's not because yesterday I told her it's not all okay. Yesterday I told her I wanted to break up. I shouldn't have done that. Now I need her, but now I have no one.

I resolve to get drunk, as soon as I can. Or visit mum, or both, she doesn't know me anymore anyway. She'll ramble away and so will I. Then one of us will break down in tears and it will all get a bit embarrassing, nursing staff wondering who started it. Shit, I need Josie. I feel for my phone in my pocket, pull it out and swipe it open. I stare at the screen. It's totally wrong, isn't it? After I had dumped her, to call her up wanting her sympathy, her attention, her shoulder to cry on? Yeah but I need her don't I? It's at times like these… and after all, I'm a selfish bastard, I must be, she told me so.

I dial up her number, press call, hold the phone to my ear. My heart is pumping hard against my ribs, a trickle of fear creeping out of my hand, down my arm, winding around my body and squeezing. Tighter and tighter as I realise I can hear her phone ringing, twenty yards behind me.

# The Mists Of Time
By Steve Kill

Over mountain and through the vale
A mist descends to shroud the land
An eerie fog before my eyes
I cannot even see my hand

Its ghostly haze is clear to me
It makes no sound as I just stare
But as I reach to touch its form
Suddenly there is nothing there

It almost seems that time stands still
As even with the brightest light
I cannot find my way within
As if the day has turned to night

And myths and magic come alive
Within the shades of white and grey
Tales of dragons, legends of old
Unicorns who enchant the way

Do they exist, using the mist?
So they can move from place to place
Hidden within the murky winds
Hiding from the human race

Given a chance to move around
Shrouded behind the misty sky
Am I dreaming of this shadow
Or has a dragon passed me by

# She'd Have Something To Say
By Tom Phelps

If Great Great Grandma could come back today
And could see life now . . . .she'd have something to say.
She wouldn't believe half the things that she'd see,
Like Television, Video and D.V.D.

She'd say, *'Life is easier, mind, than it was in my day.*
*I see the collieries have gone. Good job… sad in a way.*
*The dirt has disappeared and the dust and the grime.*
*We had to work hard to keep things clean in my time.*

*You got clothes washers, dish washers, mixers and such.*
*'Course, there's still work to do . . . but not nearly so much.*
*They don't wash the front now, don't nobody care?*
*I haven't seen a WET half circle out the front … anywhere.*

*No black-leading grates and scrubbing the floor*
*Oh no, it's easier now, than it was before.*
*No mending clothes and darning socks,*
*Only watching pictures on a square box.*

*We had no 'Hire Purchase'. No borrowing for me.*
*We didn't have much, but we managed our money.*
*If we couldn't buy something . . . . . Well . . . . so what.*
*We were brought up to be satisfied with our lot.*

I went to prayer meeting Tuesday, Sisterhood Thursday
And always, always . . . three times on Sunday
But this generation, do hardly ever go.
Some don't even go to chapel for weddings no more.

I don't know what the world is coming to, it's strange to me.
Women! . . . . Going in pubs and clubs. . . . openly?
When you talk about your neighbour, you do nothing but grouse,
Because she's for ever parking in front of your house.

If you run out of sugar, you don't nip in next door
Or the little front-room shop down the street, like before.
You got to get in your car and drive for a mile
And you think you've progressed. It makes me smile.

And Pensioners going abroad now . . . to sit by a swimming pool
We had more fun on the 'Outing' with the Sunday School.
And look you, a awful lot of people have got one bad ear.
What's that? Mobile phone? Is it? Well, well, dear, dear.

Children and young people wearing clothes worth a fortune
And their music! Horrible! Our songs had a tune!'
We had the back-kitchen, the parlour and the middle room
Now you got a kitchen and lounge. Sounds more like a hotel than a home.

The house is lovely and light now, there's no doubt,

*But you got nowhere for visitors, or for laying out.*
*You might say things is better now . . . . . . . aye, perhaps*
*But we didn't eat our dinner off our laps.*

*AND! . . . . . You got no nice warm blankets on the bed.*
*You must be freezing with that French thing . . . That DUVET! . . . instead'*
*AND . . . . . .You can't go down the back to the lavatory*
*It's all inside now . . . . . Ych-a-fi!'*

If Great Great Grandma could see . . . . McDonald's chips
She'd say, *'Well a ju ju ju, they are just little strips'*
And she'd think we are cannibals … she'd say, *'Don't tell me that*
*please.'*
If we said were going out . . . . . to eat a Chinese.

If she could hear T.V. language and see T.V slaughter
She'd say, *'Shame on you. Wash your mouth out with soap and water.'*
Oh Yes, If Great Great Grandma, could come back today
And could see life now, . . . . . She'd have something to say.

# The White Hat
By Graham Watkins

Ernest Neap shuffled forward in the queue. He didn't feel conspicuous in his raincoat and white roll necked shirt. In fact, he'd dressed like that to blend in; to merge into the crowd.

Shouts of, 'Tickets please?' galvanised the people ahead of him into action; reaching into pockets, producing iPhones and holding them up to be scanned. Ernest's ticket had cost him fifteen pounds. It was a lot of money for a pensioner like Ernest to pay but, and this was why he'd bought it, the ticket was a means of escape from his mundane life for a couple of days. The cyber security conference promised entertainment, a chance to get out of the house and perhaps even find a new career.

Since retiring, Ernest had tried working as a security guard in the shopping mall but he'd been fired after three days.

'You're too old to chase shoplifters and teenage yobs around shops Neap,' said his supervisor, 'and you should have told us about your knee replacement. Go home old man and put your slippers on.'

Cyber security, that was the answer; sitting in front of a computer would suit him fine. It never occurred to Ernest that computer programming was involved.

'Ticket!' demanded a kid in a green t-shirt on the door.

Ernest fumbled in his pocket, producing a handkerchief and a crumpled slip of paper. The bar code was a faded lemon yellow. 'My printer needs a new ink cartridge,' he explained.

The kid grinned, nudged his companion, then tried and failed to scan Ernest's paper ticket. He shrugged and gave up. The second youth handed Ernest a ribbon with a security badge and shoved a plastic bag at him.

'What's this?' asked Ernest.

'Goody bag,' replied the youth. 'Your t-shirt, programme and stuff.'

Propelled forward by the queue, Ernest stopped at a table in the atrium and rifled through the bag: A pen, chocolate bar, the programme, leaflets and a grey t-shirt. He unfolded the shirt, held it up and read, 'CyberX 2018.' Around him visitors were undressing and slipping on their grey t-shirts. It was easy for them. Most had arrived dressed in shirt and jeans. Ernest removed his coat and was about to take of his white roll necked shirt when he changed his mind. Instead he pulled the grey t-shirt on, over his white shirt and put his coat back on.

'So there it is, we're in,' said the speaker. The lecture hall was brightly lit and full. A dribble of cold sweat ran down Ernest's back. He wanted to remove his coat but there was no room to move. Tier upon tier of watchers followed the green dot as the laser light danced across the screen. Some made notes. Others used their phones to photograph the images of computer code. The auditorium buzzed with excitement. Eager to see, Ernest peered over the shoulder of the cameraman, standing in front of him.

The speaker, a young man wearing a black t-shirt with long hair wound in a bun, turned off his laser pen. 'I'm happy to take a few questions.'

Several hands shot up. The speaker scanned the sea of faces and pointed to the back of the lecture hall to a youth with large glasses. 'Brains in Thunderbirds, he'll do,' thought the speaker. The audience waited while a helper hurried up the stairs with a microphone.

'So are you saying the programme you've written will penetrate any firewall?' asked Brains.

'Yes I am,' answered the speaker, 'and, as I've just demonstrated with Mcabbey and DogGuard the firewalls are totally unaware they've been compromised.'

'What about Thornton?'

'Just as useless.' The speaker scrolled back to an earlier slide of a dozen leading firewall logos. 'They all are. If it's a computer connected to the internet no firewall is impenetrable and the claims they all make in their advertising blurb are ALL bullshit.'

In less than an hour, Ernest had watched the speaker penetrate different firewalls, undetected by the systems supposed to protect the computers. He'd exfiltrated data, installed malicious software, taken control of a network operating system, encrypted data and sent a ransom demand.

'That's about it guys. Don't worry; I'm a white hat,' said the speaker. 'What you have just seen is real but no harm has been done. Now, if I was a black hat, a hacker with evil intent, you can see how easy it would be for me to do real damage. I'll be sharing all the programme code on my website after the presentation and if you want to see it again there will also be a podcast. Feel free to use the code I've written and you're welcome to improve it but remember, we're all red team members here, our job is to test organisations defences not to break in and steal stuff.' He smiled, acknowledging the applause signalling the end of his presentation.

Ernest sat and waited while the lecture hall cleared. Young, long-haired computer geeks, unshaven, some in shredded jeans, shuffled down the stairs, past the speaker's desk and out of the hall. A few lingered to ask the speaker questions, to congratulate him and thank him for sharing the secrets that would unlock the back-door of any computer.

A podcast, available on the internet, giving away a programme, written to break into computers, struck Ernest as ridiculous; like handing out lock-picks to burglars - a hackers bonanza. Get your free crook's kit here!

He thought back to when things were simpler, when thieves used a brick or a jemmy to break in, a fishing rod through a letterbox to hook keys from a hall table, a time when real villains used sawn-offs to rob banks, a time when his mates called him Nipper Neap, a time when he had mates.

The speaker was drinking coffee in the atrium, apparently listening to a lanky kid dressed in a grey t-shirt, when Ernest approached. In fact the speaker was only half listening. The other half of his cortex was comparing the kid with Shaggy Rogers and wondering if he had a dog called Scooby Doo.

'Last year I was in the team that pen tested Buy and Save,' said the kid. 'You know, the supermarket chain.'

'Cool,' said the speaker.

'We probed with a Neutrino Exploit Kit and then did some manual stuff. It was easy. I got in through the finance director's personal laptop. Imagine that. The finance director, what a twat. His password was a joke and got me straight past the firewall and into Buy and Save's head office network. I left a little present, just to prove the hack.'

'Present, what do you mean?'

'I changed the purchasing algorithm.' The kid rubbed the stud in his nose. 'Yeah, to wind them up - ten tons of baked beans randomly ordered to different stores. It'll take them months to find out why.' He giggled nervously, waiting for a reaction; to see if we enjoyed his joke.

A convoy of lorries loaded with baked beans, thundering along a motorway, flashed though Ernest's mind.

The speaker raised his eyebrow and turned to Ernest.

Realising he'd said a stupid thing and over-stepped the mark, the kid, backed away and melted into the crowd.

'Why did you do it?' Ernest asked quietly.

'Do what?'

'You say you're a white hat but you're giving these kids the tools to hack into computers.'

The speaker placed his cup on a table and motioned for Ernest to follow. He stumbled after the speaker, pushing through the crowded foyer and out to the plaza.

The speaker turned and faced Ernest, holding his hand up to shade his eyes from the sun. 'You don't look like a programmer. Who are you?'

'I'm a security expert,' said Ernest. 'A white hat.'

'You a white hat!' said the speaker. 'Do you even know what it means?'

Ernest felt the barb. The cheeky young sod was insulting him.

'How old are you?' asked Ernest. 'Twenty, twenty-five? When you were a kid didn't you go to Saturday morning pictures?'

The speaker looked blank, as if he was listening politely but he wasn't. His cortex was thinking, 'Who is this old man? I think he looks like Uncle George.'

It occurred to Ernest that multiplex cinemas might not show Saturday morning pictures any longer. 'Every week they would show a short cowboy film and the good guy always wore a white hat....'

'Of course, we all know and guess what, Uncle George?' interrupted the speaker. 'The bad guys wore black hats.' He grinned. 'So you're telling me you were a sheriff, you tamed a town, put the bad guys in jail. I bet you even got the girl in the white dress. Don't tell me.' He put a finger to his forehead. 'She was the school teacher.'

Ernest took a small involuntary step towards him. 'I was a copper, Nipper Neap of the Yard. You might have heard of me.'

'Nipper Neap of the Yard. Well Mr. Policeman or should I say Mr. Ex Policeman, you ask a very good question. Why do I do it? I'll tell you why. This is a cyber security conference. We're here to talk about how to beat the black hats and to do that we have to learn about the tools they use, to follow them down the rabbit hole. That's why, to share the knowledge.' He checked his watch. 'I have to go. A talk I want to hear on side stepping data leak protection with just a browser is about to start... Look Columbo, if you're serious about understanding what I'm doing, check out the code. You'll find the answer there.'

'Who's Uncle George?' called Ernest but there was no reply. The speaker had gone, back into the conference centre.

Ernest spent hours looking at the programme's code but it told him nothing. He simply wasn't good enough to understand. Like an old dog, he was struggling with a new trick. The speaker had said the answer was in the code but the jumble of numbers, letters and symbols was beyond Ernest. He wasn't clever enough to unlock it, to reveal its secret.

Then, one evening, he decided to test the code, to see if it really worked, to prove the speaker's presentation wasn't fake and perhaps learn what he would not tell.

Ernest switched on his computer and ran the speaker's programme. It stopped and asked for a target. Ernest thought for a moment and then typed Goldpower.com. He wasn't sure why he chose his electricity supplier as the guinea pig. Any large company would have been suitable.

The screen went black, then, after a few seconds, it turned dark blue. Letters and numbers started to flash across the screen as if someone was typing furiously.

'What's happening,' muttered Ernest. The typing accelerated and became a blur of characters. Unsure what he was supposed to do next

Ernest went to make a cup of tea. He returned, carefully placed his cup and saucer beside the keyboard and munched on a digestive biscuit. The typing had stopped. The screen had changed. The speaker's programme had worked its magic. Ernest was in and, what's more, he had domain admin. He could go anywhere he pleased in Gold Power's computer network; customer details, suppliers records, bank accounts, policy documents, emails, nothing was hidden. Gold Power's inner secrets were his to explore.

Ernest grinned. He felt rather pleased with himself. He'd hacked into a big company. 'Cyber security isn't that hard,' he said to no one in particular.

Of course, getting in was one thing but what should he do now? Ernest didn't know. He'd not really been paying attention during that part of the speaker's presentation. Ernest wasn't a thief, he didn't want to hurt Gold Power or blackmail the company but it wouldn't do any harm to have a look around, would it?

Ernest spent more than an hour exploring. He read boring emails, minutes of meetings agreeing price increases, personnel records and then, almost by accident, he found himself looking at his own electricity account. Mr. Ernest P. Neap - estimated meter reading 16th November 268,456Kwh - units consumed 1,243Kwh balance outstanding £218.56. The paper bill had arrived from Gold Power in the post that very morning. Ernest held the invoice up against the screen and compared the amounts, half expecting them to be different. They were the same. Then, he had an idea. Why not issue himself with a credit note? No one would know. He wouldn't be greedy; a couple of hundred pounds. Gold Power could afford that.

Ernest raised the credit note for two hundred pounds and waited for his account update. Minutes passed. Nothing happened.

'Oh well! Must have done something wrong. Probably for the best,' muttered Ernest and closed the programme. He was tired and it was past his bed-time.

A loud bang woke Ernest. It was dark. Someone was breaking in. He fumbled for his glasses on the bedside table and peered at the alarm. It was five o'clock. Loud voices. Men were yelling inside the house. Heavy footsteps pounded up the stairs. The bedroom door burst open. A torch beam blinded Ernest. Strong hands pulled him up and forced his arms back. He was handcuffed and dragged from the room.

'Find his computer,' ordered a voice.

'It's here,' shouted another.

'Bring it along.'

Ernest sat in the interview room. A naked light bulb glared down. Wearing just the boxer shorts he wore in bed, he was cold and tired. The canvas chair hurt his back. Lunchtime had passed but there was no food. His stomach was growling. Ernest scratched the stubble on his chin and yawned.

'Are we boring you,' said the inspector.

Ernest stared at the inspector's bulbous red nose. He knew the type from his time in the force; beer belly bruisers who enjoyed celebrating in the police social club after a good collar.

'I'm tired.'

'Gold Power's security team knew, as soon as you were in their network. They watched you poking about, saw everything you did,' said the inspector. He smiled. Nipper Neap of the yard, a crooked cop, what a great case to crack. He'd dine out on this one. 'Thought you were clever, did you Neap, hacking their system?'

'I told you, I was testing a programme from the cyber security conference in Manchester. For God's sake, you know I'm a retired copper. I haven't done any damage. You can check.'

The inspector sat back in his chair. He was enjoying the interview, enjoying putting Nipper Neap in his place. 'You were probably scouting and planned to come back later.' He got up and went to the window. 'Do you want to know how their security knew who you were?'

'Was it because I looked at my electricity account?'

'Did you? I didn't know that,' said the inspector and sat down again. '...There was an alarm in the programme code you used. It warned them you were hacking their network and,' he pointed at Ernest, 'it did something else. The code unlocked an executable file which laid a breadcrumb trail straight back to your computer. You see, while you were hacking their network, snooping around in Gold Power's system their security team was exploring your computer. Ingenious, don't you think?'

'So what happens now? What are you going to do with me?'

'I'm going to charge you and, you'll be pleased to know, the courts are cracking down on cyber crime. Ernest Neap, an ex copper hacking into a major utility's computer network. They'll love that. You might not have stolen anything but you'll get a custodial sentence. Three to five years, I should say,' said the inspector.

Three to five! Ernest felt sick.

'You're not the first,' smirked the inspector.

'What do you mean I'm not the first?'

'Honey-pot has caught other black hats with their hands in the till.'

'Honey-pot, what's honey-pot?' asked Ernest but he already knew the answer; it was in the code. Then he remembered, honey-pot was the name of the speaker's programme.

Ernest Neap was home on bail, waiting for a trial date, when there was a knock at the front door.

'Looks official,' said the postman and handed him a brown envelope together with a second, white envelope. Ernest recognised the Crown Prosecution Service Crest on the corner of the brown envelope. His heart sank as he signed for the letter. He took the letters into the kitchen, carefully slit the brown envelope open, read the contents and did a little dance around the kitchen table.

Because of his exemplary record as a decorated police officer with many years of service and because no harm had been done the CPS had decided to drop all charges against him. 'His activity, penetration testing Gold Power Limited, was considered by the CPS to be the action of a White Hat,' said the letter.

In the excitement he forgot the white envelope was there. Later that morning while he was preparing a celebration lunch, a sausage sandwich with brown sauce, he found it on the table.

The envelope was from Gold Power Limited. In it was a single sheet of paper, a credit note issued by their accounts department for two hundred pounds.

# Flora's Bag
## By Helen Adam

Flora looked slowly round the decorated function room, checking all details were perfect. White flowers were on all the tables, with wedding favours of tiny cakes, handmade chocolates and smooth pebbles in bags. The crystal ware was gleaming. Each and every chair had its own little decorative coat, complete with bow.

It all looked exactly how Naomi, today's demanding bride, had specified...'shabby chic, but a bit lux, you know what I mean? And lots of little touches to spoil my guests'.

Flora's head ached and her cheeks were tired from smiling at Naomi and her extended family, but she had more details to check.

Lingering briefly by a table in the corner...those chocolate favours were so cute... she suddenly felt she had to take one. She had ordered just the right number for the guests, but, hey, if there were one missing, no one would notice, surely. Lots got left behind after most events. Guests, already sated on food, were careless after a few sparkling glasses.

A small bag of chocolates casually dropped itself into her bag as she left the table, almost by accident it seemed. On her way through the room, a couple of glass candle holders belonging to the hotel also landed inside, and a delicate silk scarf, (maybe it was hers after all), hanging forgotten on a coat stand, was also tidied away as she passed through to check the pre dinner drinks.

Much later that night, as she scrabbled through the bag for her front door key, her hands found this haul. A second's confused guilt was replaced by mild elation. She slipped off her shoes with relief, and put on the kettle, already unwrapping and biting into the chocolate that somehow, she wasn't sure how, was there just when she needed it. Later, she found herself sifting small, smooth and so satisfying white pebbles through her fingers... over and over again, until they began to soothe the ache in her head.

Tomorrow was another day and another wedding. This one needed more work, and she was soon busy arranging to collect the bunches of freesias, rice paper confetti, name cards and harpist in the morning. As she did, familiar sensations overwhelmed her. Hunger, resentment, and an intense yearning ache. All these women, these damn brides, they had families, husbands to be, they had money for hotel suites and honeymoons, and yet they still wanted doves, flowers, tiny cakes, and potted lavenders. And Flora wanted them too. Maybe there would be no family, no smug adoring man, no loving if slightly tedious parents, no line of best friends in lilac satin for her; but there could be sweet tasting treats, sparkles of luxury, all the little gifts of love. No one could say she didn't deserve them.

Over the next six months her little flat began to fill up with treasure; a pair of cream silk cushions from a penthouse flat, a bowl of succulents from a time faded mansion, countless tea lights and candles and cut glass holders, and even a live baby white rabbit, (one of ten released at a croupier's wedding), all spent time at the bottom of her bag. She supped most nights on fondant fancies, bags of pick and mix, salmon and cream cheese sandwiches, and tiny bottles of wine, all artfully and semi consciously lifted as she moved about her busy successful days, planning and titivating wedding after wedding. The rabbit too, enjoyed crudities; ornamental cabbage and cottage garden flowers, and greeted the thud of her leather bag on the floor with twitching nosed interest.

Petting him goodbye in late December, Flora set off for a midwinter wedding with a sense of slight foreboding. It was probably just the dark and lashing rain, but she felt edgy as she arrived at the country hotel. Less than usually adept as she knocked some miniature gold glazed pies off the elaborately arranged tea table and into her bag, she hooked curious glances too from a couple of the kitchen staff. Less light-fingered than usual, she fumbled the place names, and then stumbled over her instructions to the best man. Her mind was taken over by her need to survey the room for small items to take; to hide them away, to steal. It had become a compulsion. She knew she had no need or even wish to possess yet another coloured glass candleholder, but three more found themselves slipped into her ever-fattening bag.

Just before the cake was cut, all the guests were gathered, and she stood with them, under the hotel's towering and expensively decorated tree, a cut spruce at least thirty feet tall. The evening had reached that point of happy drunken no return and was about to slide into the records as another organisational success, despite her earlier forebodings. With half her attention on the bride's mother who was kissing her new son in law, as he stood poised with his hand on the knife that would plunge into the icy heart of his and his new wife's fantasy cake, she let her left hand reach out to the tree. It landed on a glass-mirrored bauble that swung and sparkled and reflected the room irresistibly.

Keeping her eye on the couple, soon to be joined together forever through the ritual of cake, her fingers began to twist and prise this delightful thing from its branch. One part of her brain was already calculating that there was just room in her bag, (her capable and capacious bag), for another item. On top of the arctic fur throw, the beaded reindeer, the whisky chocolates, and the tartan covered boxes; there was still room for one more thing.

As she finally released the coveted item from the needles in which it had become entangled, smiling rather stiffly at the wedding group, she felt a shaking above her, and the tree began to sway. Rendered unstable by her fumbling, the foliage shifted, creaked, and began to scatter tinsel and lights, glass snowflakes, chocolate coins, and a myriad of gaudy items. The overwrought tree became increasingly unstable and creaked as it scattered more and more; all the sparkly tiny objects she could ever collect, a perfect storm of gifts, landed on her, and the bride and groom. As it finally fell, it cracked open the edifice of their elaborate cake, and shrilly scattered the perfectly posed group. Flora's still open bag was knocked from her arm, emptying its contents at her feet.

The reflective bauble that she held in her hand slipped from her grasp and it bounced away down the room. Flora could see herself reflected in its many sides: her past, her present and her future laid bare in front of the now dumb struck guests. Its final bounce was the last sound in a room that had settled into silence, stillness after the storm. It was a small forlorn sound, and Flora caught a last glimpse of her white face and wild eyes. Other eyes were on her too; eyes that were seeing: not just the contents of her bag, but the contents of her soul, suddenly and openly in full view.

# Stone/Paper/Knife
### By Daisy Hufferdine

The three boys crashed through the school gate. 'Last one to the stone is stinky,' yelled Chris. They took the two steps down to the cinder track in one gigantic leap, and then sprinted diagonally across the village green.

Kevin was struggling, his feet slopping around in his sisters red and pink wellies. 'Not fair,' he yelled 'I've lost my shoes.' Mike brought up the rear as they raced down the ginnel between Grandma Clark's and Mr.Stowell's houses. In truth, he would never win any race. Mike wasn't built for speed.

'Stinky, stinky,' chorused the duo, as Mike ambled towards the large boulder. They were triumphantly dancing across the top.

He smirked, 'My shoes are clean, my feet are dry and my homework is not scattered all over the green'. Mike was built with brains.

The Stone was the meeting place for the gang, a huge glacial conglomerate encased in the river embankment. The top was level with the field. A great place to sit and make up pirate stories. A sheer triangular monolith of rock faced the river, a good spot to hide away. Chris was a farmer's son and had *Bomber*. On his fourteenth birthday his Uncle Joe had given him a penknife which he had brought down to the Stone. 'It's got twelve blades,' he boasted. It looked like a vicious scorpion, a red cross emblazoned on its back, with tools and blades stretching in all directions. It was the place where they put their plans together. In Year 9. Brian Quinn had been terrorising

Mike in the school playground. One look at Bomber and a gentle suggestion was enough for Brian.

'Why do you call it bomber?' asked Kevin, as Chris was chiselling their initials into the stone.

'Cause it's mine.'

That wasn't their only discovery in Year 9. One Friday morning on the school bus, Kevin instructed the others to meet at noon tomorrow. He had a glint in his eyes. The others suspected that he wanted to talk about the Sex Ed class they had on Wednesday. After a prompt arrival, he placed a blue packet in front of them.

'What is it?' asked Mike.

'Pick it up, have a read,' instructed Kevin.

'It says *Hercules* on one side and *Tutti Frutti* on the other.'

Chris took it, 'It's slippy and bumpy and smells funny. Shall I slice it open with Bomber?'

'No' yelled Kevin.'

'Where did you get it?'

'Found it.'

They stood around, not sure what to do next.

'I'm going home for m' dinner,' said Chris.

'No, wait, just pull open the top' pleaded Kevin.

Chris picked up the packet and a large, irradiance, ribbed condom spilled onto the stone, a smell of strawberries and pineapple filled the air.

'WOW,' said all three boys together.

Mike prodded it with a stick. 'It's not like the one Miss put on the carrot.'

'You could fit a marrow in there,' said Kevin. His father was a gardener.

'Perhaps they use it on the bulls,' suggested Chris.

By Year 11 Mike was regularly completing all their Maths homework. 'What are you two going to do in the exams?' he demanded.

'Doesn't matter,' said Chris. 'I'm going to leave at the end of the year and work with Dad on the farm.'

Kevin was quiet, 'I'm leaving too', he announced. 'I'm going to join the navy and see the world.'

'Hang on' said Mike,' You can't swim.'

'I'm going to be a chef, and get all the action I want. I don't need to swim. They have big boats. What about you? Are you going to work for your Dad at the cement works?'

'Yea, sort of,' replied Mike. 'I want to get a degree, then I will be able to work in their research department.'

'How long will that take?' asked Chris.

'Another five years.'

'That's tough,' said Kevin. 'I could be a Master Chef by then.'

'Or, you could be dead,' said Mike quietly.

Three years later Kevin was home on shore leave. He sent a message to the others. *See you at the Stone at 7.30pm.* As Mike and Chris approached, Kevin was stood on the top of the rock in a large black coat.

'What's he wearing?' Chris whispered to Mike.

'I think it is part of his uniform. Maybe he thinks he's Horatio Nelson.'

'Ugh. Who?'

'Hi boys.' He made a mock salute in their direction.

'It's mid-summer Kev, why are you wearing your coat?' asked Chris.

'To hide my surprise, ta-da.'

He flung back the front opening to reveal a huge sheaf knife strapped to his leg. 'Boys say hello to Bertha, Bertha say hello to my mates.'

Chris, being a polite farmer's son was just about to mouth hello when Mike's elbow jarred into his ribs, taking his breath away. Instead, an ow sound emerged which Kevin interpreted as 'wow.'

'Where did you get it?' asked Mike

' We were on a joint exercise in and around the Hawaiian Islands. I got it in Honolulu. It was the biggest and sharpest I could find.'

'It is a monster,' agreed Mike.

'Yeah, you could butcher a pig with that,' said Chris. 'Mind you, you would need Bomber to finish off.'

'Ugh,' said Mike.

Their lives continued with occasional meetings; at Christmas, at Chris and Susie's wedding, at Kevin's father's funeral. Chris had a big birthday party in February which Mike attended, Kevin was at Sea and sent apologies. They all agreed to meet up next time he was home. Mike's birthday was in June. He didn't want a party, his parents secretly planned a family gathering. Mike hated every minute of it. What was there to celebrate? Getting through another year of hard slog, writing paper after paper. Everyone said that he was on track to achieve a First, providing his dissertation came up to scratch. More pressure, why did they do that?

News arrived that Kevin would be home on the Second of August, Chris and Susie's baby was due on the tenth, Mike planned to have his synopsis completed. The days and nights rumbled on. Despite endless beginnings he couldn't settle on a theme. He couldn't find anything original or interesting he wanted to write up despite the numerous concoctions of coffee, whiskey and uppers. Instead, a different plan was occupying his mind. After years and years listening to Chris and Kevin brag of their trophies, it was his turn and he knew exactly what he was going to do. It would take careful planning, precise timing, courage and strength.

Kevin's confirmation text came through on the thirtieth of July, *lets meet at five o'clock in the pub.*

Quickly Mike replied, *Can we make it five at the Stone, I have a surprise for you both?*

*Sure, just like old times,* texted Kevin.

*Suits me, what have you got up your sleeve?* enquired Chris.

Mike nearly laughed aloud when he read their texts, the irony of the words. He woke early on the second morning, his mother brought up tea and toast shortly after eight. He quickly shut down his computer. 'Can you use a PC Mum?' he asked.

'Me, goodness no, your Dad does all that stuff at work, in his office.'

'It's easy once your in, you just have to remember your password. I use irene123, all lower case. I won't forget that.'

She smiled, it was her name. She ruffled his hair and closed the door gently.

Mike sighed, 'Courage and strength, courage and strength'. The words were his mantra. He lay down on his bed. He could feel his treasure under the pillow. The food sat untouched. Shortly after three he decided to get dressed. He would need something smart, that would surprise Chris and Kevin. He choose a black shirt and trousers with a royal blue jumper. He turned both cuffs inside, that would give him a secure hiding place. He put the toast and tea down the toilet, then washed the cup and plate. He tidied his room, all papers and files neatly stacked, bed made and clothes placed in his wardrobe. He left the PC switched on but turned the monitor off. He slid his hand under the pillow and carefully retrieved the kitchen vegetable knife. The sharpened blade sparkled in the sunlight. 'Come on Stinky, we can do this.'

As expected he was the first to arrive. Sitting on the Stone was so peaceful, not even squabbling ducks to break the silence. Carefully he withdrew the knife from his sleeve. 'Well, what do you think of your name? You must think it's okay. I don't care, it's been mine since I was nine years old. You will meet Bertha and Bomber today. Don't let them intimidate you. You're just as good as they are, better in fact, cause you're mine.'

'I'm so tired Stinky, nothing ever works for me. I haven't got a single line written of my dissertation, not even an idea. The only place I've been to is Preston Uni and that's boring. I've never had a girlfriend, I'm not funny or smart. I'm just boring old Mike who knows where to find books in the library.' He scratched his wrists as the words came tumbling out. 'We will have to listen to Kevin rattle on about the *Hercules* map of his conquests, telling us what he has seen and done. Chris will be boasting how much the farm is worth and how one day it will be all his. 'Will either of them ask about my life, will they ask about what I have done? So much for mates'.

He picked up the vegetable knife, moving it from one hand to the other. 'But you will help me Stinky, courage and strength'. Quickly he took the knife in his right hand and slit his left wrist. The blood pumped out. He turned the blade around and dipped the handle in the pool that had collected by his leg. 'We must tell them who you are.' He wrote STINKY in large letters on the stone.

# The Angelystor Of Llangernyw
## By Graham Watkins
### Previously published in his book 'Welsh Legends and Myths.'

*'When the bell begins to toll,*
*Lord, have mercy on the soul.'*

*The Venerable Bede, 672-735.*

In days past, when good and evil were known to be two sides of the same coin, people feared the devil. They understood that Satan and his followers congregated around churches, hoping to steal souls. Devils and demons, it was believed, were afraid of the sound of bells. In Ireland, evil spirits were driven away by the ringing of church bells. The same is true in Scotland. In Wales, the mournful toll of a church bell, known as the passing bell, would start when a person was on their death bed. During the funeral, the church bell was often accompanied by the ringing of a second, smaller, hand bell. This corpse bell, as it was known, would be carried in front of the body, as it was carried to its final resting place, to protect the soul of the dead person from Satan.

Many Welsh churches were built with north and south facing doors. Before a funeral or christening, the north door would be opened but then the priest would enter through the south door. The north door, commonly known as the devil's door, would remain open during the service so that evil spirits in the church could flee from the ringing bells they hated so much.

Despite these and other precautions, evil spirits were still a problem in churches. One church with a particularly unpleasant kind of demon was St. Dygain's in the village of Llangernyw. The demon was an Angelystor or 'Recording Angel' so named because, at the stroke of midnight each All-Hallows Eve, the demon would whisper the names of those who would pass away in the coming year.

When a new tailor named Shon Ap Robert moved into the village he was amused to learn about the messenger of death that haunted the church. Shon was a strong, confident young fellow, full of life and always ready for some fun.

'An Angelystor you call it, who can foretell the future. What nonsense. I don't believe in spirits,' he said one evening in the tavern.

'Don't scoff at things you don't understand,' warned his drinking companions. As the evening passed and more ale flowed, Shon grew bolder.

'I'll prove there's no such thing, this very Halloween, by waiting in the church until the clock strikes twelve,' said Shon.

'Don't be a fool,' replied the landlord.

'Leave the Angelystor in peace if you value your soul,' said another.

'How much do you wager that I will hear no names?' challenged Shon with a swagger.

'I will stake five shillings that you will hear the names and those people will be dead within the year,' said a drinker by the bar.

'I accept your wager,' cried Shon.

Every day the villagers tried to dissuade the tailor from his quest. The priest warned him it was a mistake. The doctor told Shon he was a fool and the tavern keeper, frightened for the young man's sanity, tried to stop him.

'A bet has been made and, as a man of principle, I am obliged to honour it,' replied the confident tailor and would not be swayed.

October passed quickly and late on All-Hallows Eve he entered the church alone. His solitary candle flickered, casting strange dancing shadows on the walls. Shon ap Robert sat quietly on a pew, near the altar and waited. Outside, the great yew that grew in the churchyard was being buffeted by the wind. Shon held his pocket watch up to the candle. It was ten minutes to twelve. Slowly, the minutes ticked past. The cold church air was chilling Shon to his very marrow and he felt less confident than he had done that convivial evening in the tavern.

'Even if I hear a name, it cannot harm me,' said Shon to himself and waited nervously in the gloom. There was a bang and the door of the church burst open. A gust of wind blew out Shon's candle. Then, the door slammed shut, leaving Shon in darkness.

'Who's there,' shouted Shon but there was no reply. Instead, he heard something shuffling across the floor. Shon wanted to jump up and flee but the church was dark as ink and he had no idea where the door was. He sat as if riveted to the pew.

'Shon Ap Robert, Shon Ap Robert,' whispered a voice, close by. Shon could feel putrid breath near his face.

'Hold. Hold. I'm not ready,' cried the tailor and fumbled for a match.

'Shon Ap Robert,' whispered the voice again. He struck the match. There was no one there. He was alone in the church. Shon looked at his watch. It was one minute past twelve.

The people were shocked the following morning, when they saw the tailor. His hair had turned white and his face was wrinkled with age.

'Did you see the Angelystor?' asked the villagers.

'I saw nothing,' replied Shon.

'Tell us. Did he whisper the names?' asked the priest.

'Just one,' replied Shon and wearily handed over the five shillings he had wagered.

Shon Ap Robert never told the people of Llangernyw who the messenger of death had named that fearful night but, when he died within the year, they knew. The little parish church was packed for the funeral of Shon Ap Robert and, as he was laid to rest, the corpse bell was rung loudly to protect the soul of the unfortunate tailor who had so rashly dared to challenge the Angelystor.

# Walking With A Dead Horse
By Stella Starnes

It was my father who suggested that we should attend the Mari Lywd festival in Llanwrtyd Wells on New Year's Eve.

It was the day after Boxing Day. I was in Tirabad on a cold winter's morning. Smoky grey clouds obscured the sun and muffled the sky like a thick, fluffy blanket. Now I was ensconced in a chair in my Dad's blood orange kitchen.

'It'll be fun Ella,' he said, as I ate my toast and peanut butter. 'We'll walk through the streets in a procession, very late at night, holding flaming torches while someone dressed as a dead horse leads the way, and at the end, we get to have a glass of wine and mince pies at the Abernant Hotel.'

I swallowed my third piece of toast and picked up my fourth. At the same time, the impact of what he was saying suddenly hit me and it fell back on the plate.

'What, we have something to eat and drink as if it doesn't matter that we've been following something dead, in the dark?!' I said. The very idea of it made my stomach churn, like the poisoned remains of Ceridwen's magic brew in a big black cauldron. I felt sick. I wished I'd finished all of my toast before he'd mentioned the dead horse bit.

The smile on his face faltered. I drew a deep breath. It was an unfortunate habit of his to jump unexpected outings on me. I had a certain fear of close contact with the dead, too. The idea of it being in the dark of the night would only make it seem more real. Did he really think I would find that fun? I didn't think so.

'Yeah, it sounds real fun honey,' said Melanie, my dad's girlfriend, with her usual American twang, as she walked into the kitchen. She was always up for an outing, however unexpected it might be. She was already bouncing on the balls of her feet. 'Although I have to say I feel rather sorry for the horse too,' she added.

'Yes, quite,' I agreed. The idea that someone would dress up as a dead animal filled me with horror.

'Why on earth would anyone want to disguise themselves like that though?' I asked. 'I mean, I know it's a costume, but what if the person wearing it has got something to hide? What if they're a bit dodgy?'

Dad looked at me.

'No, they're not. It's not a disguise sweetie. The leader wouldn't dream of hurting anyone. It doesn't matter that he carries the skull of a horse either: the animal is long dead; it doesn't know any better', he said. He scratched his silvery grey beard. 'We can at least see what the festivity is like.'

'Yeah, sure,' said Melanie as she noticed the tears standing in my eyes, 'but someone would have kept the horse's head for such a festivity rather like a trophy and used it more than once, with no thought for the poor beast when it was alive and trotting. Is that any way to treat the dead, never mind that it's a horse?'

I shook my head. I hated the idea of making sport of and holding onto the remains of anything dead. It could as easily be any other animal's head, or, if it were a cannibal's carnival, my own head. I shuddered.

However, when I went back home the next day, Irene, a Christian friend of mine said, 'Dear me, girl, your face is as white as a sheet!' as she looked up from her laptop on the dining room table. 'Here, I've made you some tea,' and she handed me a steaming mugful. I sipped it gratefully.

I sat down in an armchair and she peered at me in interest. Holding the cup between both hands, I told her about Dad's idea of how to hail the New Year.

'Your Dad really should have explained it to you,' she said afterwards. 'It's true that the Mari Lwyd Festival is an old traditional event here in Wales but considering that the dead horse costume includes the horse's skull it almost sounds horrible enough to be a Halloween outfit. You know I can't abide Halloween. All of the costumes look like the living dead. The skeletal figure of any animal, let alone a horse, is a dark, ungodly image so soon after the birth of Christ.'

'Yeah, I agree. The sight of an outfit like that in a shop encourages people to think it's cool to look ugly,' I said. 'Nothing at Christmastime should ever look ugly.'

'You're right Ella,' Irene said, and she gave me a broad smile. 'Well, you don't have to go if you don't want to. You can always say no.'

'I know.' I smiled back.

I could have said no, but when I picked up the phone and called Dad, I didn't. After all, I had to admit that it was, as Irene had said, a unique Welsh custom so it wouldn't do any harm to see what significance this festival held.

New Year's Eve was now upon us. Dad, Melanie and I got out of the car in the car park of Llanwrtyd Wells. The time was 8.30 in the evening. The sky was dark velvet blue and the air was chilly. We walked up to the town square, which was crowded with people all wrapped up in coats, hats and scarves. They were all holding what looked like long wooden clubs in their hands, until I saw a striking of many matches and heard the crackle of flames as the torches blazed up. *Oh, yes, the torches!* I thought, and for a moment I was transfixed by the fire as it danced like dozens of red hot demons in the darkness. Suddenly I found that I, too, was being presented with a torch and I wondered if we were going on a witch hunt, but who would we be setting ablaze?

The Mari, an old grey beast whose coat was as white as a death shroud and with its long, bony head held high, all festooned with bright red, pink and yellow ribbons as if in mockery of its long lost, living mane, led us onward and out of the square. It trotted down a dry, earthy farm track. We all followed in silence, like stealthy hunters, our torches illuminating our pale faces, pinched by the cold wintry breeze. I looked up at it, and it looked sideways at me, but as much those empty, soulless eyes provoked my pity the overall image of its dead white skull in all of its boniness against the pitch black, moonless night also frightened me.

Suddenly, we all spotted a dark, robed figure walking up towards us on the path and it spoke with a booming voice. 'May God have mercy on you all!' it cried. 'Turn your torches on this devilish imposter! Flee; flee you ignorant cowards, for it is your holy duty to escape from this unholy demon and leave it burning before it takes you back where it belongs!'

For me this was both a sound warning and the last straw as I watched this tall, imposing minister make the sign of the cross as if to ward away the Mari Lwyd like a bad spirit. Yet for all of his efforts, the Mari Lwyd and the rest of the procession pushed past and I had no choice but to follow if I didn't want to be left behind. However, I saw the fear and anger in his face in the light of the torches as he noticed that there were children in the procession and it suddenly hit me that these children and I were no longer safe and sound at home, where our families would be toasting the New Year and Death did not follow Herne the Hunter into the house. I was outside on a dark moonless night walking in the wake of a man whose costume had shaken a man of the church so much that, to my own eyes (and maybe even to the some of the children), it had now come startling to life as a horse from Hell under what should have felt like a peaceful Welsh Heaven.

At last, we reached the Abernant Hotel, a pristine, marble white building that stood in front of a dank, murky lake. The bright golden electric light threw its rays out onto the gravelly drive. I sighed with relief.

Dad took out his camera. "How about a photo?"

'Yeah, sure.' I raised my burning torch. I smiled. I was standing in front of the beautiful hotel, full of life and light, and its gold, Heavenly radiance warmed my soul.

The wine and the mince pies went down a treat. I stuffed the pastries into my mouth, anything for some comfort food, and I savoured the taste of the boozy fruit. The wine felt like a balm to my soul as I quenched my thirst. It was also my wassail to the New Year. Dad, Melanie and I didn't stay to join in the singing. Instead, the photo Dad took still stands on a shelf in his house to commemorate the event.

However, I have since found that I'd been yearning to travel still further from the myriad of grass green paths, that twisted through Celtic tales, like knotted grasses and plaited plant stems to one more chapter. In the present time in a Wales that was and will always be as loyal to its myths and traditions as it is to the Royal Welsh Show and its Christian heritage.

# Sam
## By Ciaran O Connell

They lived together in a tiny terraced house on the outskirts of a small town. He collected trolleys at the local supermarket. Not a demanding job, but quite an achievement for Sam. 'He's a bit slow,' is how his mother would explain it whenever anybody asked.

The previous Tuesday, he'd come home from work and found her on the kitchen floor. She was on her back fighting to breathe. She looked up at him, her face twisted in pain.

She pushed three words out between shallow gasps. 'Slipped. Call ambulance.'

By then Sam had his fist in his mouth, biting his knuckles and rocking back and forth.

Her eyes stared at him, pleading.

'Oh Mum, I don't know what to do,' He cried as he walked around and around in a circle.

She reached out and tugged at the hem of his trousers. She pointed to the telephone, every breath struggling to make it into and out of her lungs. 'Nine… nine… nine.' The words came out as whispers.

'Oh yeah, I know.' His face lit up. 'I know what to do.' 'I have to dial nine, nine, nine but only in an emergency. Is this an emergency Mum?'

She nodded and managed another word. 'Ambulance.'

He dialled the numbers and tried to remember what he was supposed to say.

'This is 32 Coombe Terrace. My name is Sam Hunter.' He spoke slowly in a singsong voice. 'We need an ambulance please.'

She watched his face frown in concentration as he listened to the voice on the other end of the line.

'It's my mum.'

More silence.

'I don't know. She's lying on the floor. Can you come please?'

The operator grasped the situation quickly. She asked a few more questions. Ten minutes later the ambulance arrived and took Sam's mum to hospital. They took him along too.


'Your mother fractured her ankle when she fell. But she fell,' they said, 'because she had a serious lung infection.' So they kept her in.

They let Sam stay with her that first night. The next morning she made him sit in a chair facing her. His mother spoke slowly. She told him how he could get from the hospital back home. She went over it three times and then made him say it all back to her three times.

'Turn right out of the hospital then up the big hill, past the park, and the next left was the other end of Coombe Terrace. I've got it mum.' He beamed. 'I've got it mum, I've got it.'

'I must do what Mum says,' He told himself as he reached their front door and let himself in with his key. 'She needs me.'

Sam ate his bowl of cornflakes and went to work. When he got home that evening, he ate a few digestive biscuits. 'Mum said it was okay.' Then he started for the hospital.

On his way he had to pass Avery Park. As he walked alongside the park railings he heard a harsh cawing above him. A crow was perched on the top of the park gates. He hated crows. They looked at each other for a moment, then the crow took off, veering back and up toward a giant oak tree. That was when he saw the bike hanging high among the branches. The frame was bright yellow, the handlebars post-box red, and the saddle a shiny black. As he carried on his way to the hospital the beautiful bike in the tree kept popping into his head and making him smile.

At the hospital his mum told him that she was going to be all right but that she would have to stay for a few more days. He smiled at the news. It was okay, and he knew the way now.

She gave him money from her purse, and a shopping list. 'Go to the Spar on the corner, Son. Mr Ackroyd will still be open. Give him the money and the list. He'll give you the shopping. You can put it away when you get home. You know where everything goes don't you?'

He nodded. When he left the hospital he went to the Spar on the corner of his road, got the shopping from Mr Ackroyd and put it all away before he went to bed.

The next day was Thursday. On his way to the hospital that evening he stopped at the park gates and looked up at the bicycle. He walked up to the tree and stood searching the confusion of leaves and branches over his head. He spotted three faded ropes– one tied to each side of the handlebars, and one tied to the saddle. He watched it swinging in a graceful arc and he smiled. The sight of the bike gave him a warm glow in his stomach. Usually Sam hated looking up.

In his head he could hear his Dad's voice. 'Come on son, I'll give you a lift. Climb up on the crossbar. Don't worry. It'll be okay.'

They used to go out on his bike, and hare down country lanes. Sam always felt safe with his dad's two strong arms steering the bike and protecting him.

But that all changed when he was twelve. It was early in the summer. The weather had been so good and his dad had decided to walk home from his office instead of waiting for the ever-crowded bus. He was five minutes from their house when he was knocked over by a truck. He died instantly. That was ten years ago and Sam still missed him. But the bike in the tree took him back to those happy days.

He walked on to the hospital. The warm feeling stayed with him. He knew his mum would be okay now. And he was right.

'They say I'm getting better son.' She held his hand as he sat beside her. He was eating his way through the box of chocolates that Mr Ackroyd had given him for her.

'I might be home next week.' She watched him pick out his favourites. 'I shall need you to help at home young man.'

He nodded. The box was nearly empty. It was early evening and visiting hours were coming to a close. He gave her a kiss and headed home. Friday, Saturday, and Sunday all went the same way.

And then it was Monday. As he did every evening since she had been taken in, he held off looking up at the bike until he was a few yards from the park entrance. He counted the cracks in the pavement until the stone pillar of the gates showed up on the edge of his vision. Three more steps and only then did he look up into the dense foliage of the ancient oak tree. The bicycle was in its usual place.

'Everything is going to be okay,' he told himself, feeling the warmth flood through his body.

Sam carried on his way, a smile now stretching from ear to ear. It didn't occur to him to wonder why it was there, he was simply pleased to see it each evening on his way to the hospital.

'It was there again today Mum.'

'What was son?' She had slept very little that night. The woman opposite kept moaning about garden gnomes, and when she did eventually drop off around three, a nurse woke her up half an hour later to give her another dose of antibiotics.

'The bicycle. The one I told you about. The one in the tree.'

She smiled at her only son. 'Tell me again Sam. It's this medicine. I keep forgetting things.'

That evening as visiting hours came to a close hHe gave her a kiss and headed home.

It was still light when he passed the park. He looked up. He couldn't see the bike. He stared up at the tree, searching through the leaves and branches. It was definitely gone. And it was getting dark.

'Oh no. Something bad is going to happen to Mum. I've got to go back.'

'Sorry lad, you can't come in now.' The security guard was adamant when he got to the hospital entrance. 'Let your mum have her sleep. You can see her tomorrow.'

'But the bike's gone. Something bad is happening.' Sam wailed.

'What bike? Has someone stolen your bike?

'No! Not my bike. The one in the tree.'

This confused the man even more.

'Sorry son, I'm not with you. Best be off home now.'

Sam stood on the steps of the hospital and began to cry loudly.

'Stop that now. Get off home with you or I'll report you for being a nuisance.'

Sam walked home. He went straight to bed. He woke up a lot and worried a lot. The next morning he went to work. The park was in the opposite direction so he couldn't check if the bike had come back.

'What the matter Sam?' His manager, Bill, had been very encouraging when Sam started working there and took a special interest in making sure the lad was okay.

'The bike's gone.' Sam tried to explain.

'I didn't think you had a bike?'

'Of course I don't have a bike!' Sam stamped his foot. 'It's the one in the tree. It's gone. Bad things are going to happen.'

'Sorry Sam, I don't follow you.'

The day went badly. He was terrified that he would get to the hospital only to find that his mum wouldn't be coming home after all. Who would take care of him then?

When he got home from work he didn't want any biscuits. He changed his clothes and headed straight off to see his mum.

'It'll be there. It'll be there,' he told himself as he got closer and closer to the park. But there was no bike in the tree. He carried on, dread growing within him at every step. He trudged his way past a row of shops, looking down at the pavement. A man rushed from one of the doorways and crashed into him.

'Oops. Sorry son. Are you okay?'

Sam looked up at a smiling black face, all grey stubble and a stubby black nose. Long dreadlocks were topped off with a multi-coloured woolly hat and a scarf to match. Sam gazed over the man's shoulder and broke into a wide grin. There was the bike, sitting in the shop window.

'The bike. It's here!'

The man turned to the window, and then looked back to Sam.

'Of course it's here.' He let out a loud happy laugh. 'This is where it lives.'

'But why isn't it in the tree?'

'Hey, I know your face. You're one of those who spotted it right?' The man's grin grew wider. 'Good on you boy. You're in hallowed company. I put it in the tree two weeks ago. Did it late at night. A couple of my mates helped me. We borrowed a cherry picker from the Council.'

'But why?'

'It's part of The Art Among the People thing. The Council's been running it. The lamp on the handlebars was a webcam. We've been recording everybody who spotted it. You were the best. You kept looking up at it and smiling. As if it was an old friend. I'm Jonah by the way.'

Sam didn't understand but he was happy to see the bike. He knew his mum would be all right, now that he had found the bike again.

# Then Silence

## By Sally Spedding

The smells hit him first. Pee, cabbage and something else so thick he could almost taste it. The boy held his breath as he went to Birchfield House's Reception area with its two glowing heaters swivelling from side to side creating a cosy warmth. Where no-one bothered to look up.

'It's me,' he began. 'Stephen Ball. From the comp.' He drummed his nail-bitten fingers on the polished desk, until a plump nurse wearing a tight-fitting uniform finally swivelled round from her PC.

'The comp? You mean Weston Favell?'

'Yeah. 'I've come to see… ' he extracted a tightly folded sheet of school notepaper and opened it out. 'Someone called Beryl. Miss Duffy from school sorted it.'

'Ah.' The uniform took the sheet of paper and conferred with the screen. 'Mrs. Beryl Purselove.' She looked up. 'But her husband's dead and she's totally blind. Did you know?'

Miss Duffy hadn't told him that. Otherwise he'd not have bothered washing his hair or chosen a less mucky school shirt.

'And bedridden.' The nurse saved her file and sighed. 'We have other inmates who might…'

'Inmates?' he repeated, puzzled.

'I mean 'residents.''

'As I said, we have several… '

'No. I've come to see 'er.'

She rummaged in a drawer then pushed a list of names towards him under the grille.

Beryl Purselove's was, for some reason, highlighted in fluorescent green, but there was no time to ask why.

'Your signature, please.' The nurse pointed at the empty space next to it. 'You'll be her first visitor, and I think it's best if it's just the once.' She eyed the sheet of paper, then slipped it into her pocket. 'I'll tell your Miss Duffy we have a perfectly adequate quota of helpers here at Birchfield House. That we had an inspection only last June and scored almost a hundred percent.' She scrutinised his third-hand duffel coat, then the scuffed trainers. 'However, now you're here, you'd better come along.'

Those same smells and a chill intensified as one unheated corridor led to another, less well lit than the one before. Stephen knew all about how darkness saved electricity. His Dad went on about nothing else. And their 'phone, now cut off...

Having suddenly stopped without warning, that nurse's large, soft body met his, and while she hunted in her pocket for what he presumed was a key, he wanted to run. But Miss Duffy, his Year Head, was the only teacher who'd shown him any interest. Had even called round to get him back in time for the Mock exams. She'd tried alright, like his Mum would have done.

'Here we are. Number fifty three,' muttered the nurse, but its lock proved stiff. Her irritation growing with each attempt to enter.

'Let me have a go.' Stephen noticed his hand was shaking, but finally the door nudged open to an even deeper gloom and a startled cry from within.

'Who's here? Tell me!'

'She always does that,' the nurse said flatly, 'even though she's known us for ages.'

However, the wailing continued, seeming louder once the gap had widened.

'What's up with 'er?' Stephen panicked. 'For Chrissake, do somethin'!'

But the nurse ignored him and switched on the one wall light, whose dingy bulb made little difference to the gloom.

'Someone here to see you, Beryl. It's Stephen.'

'Who?' That same voice trembled.

'You heard the first time. It's Stephen.' She let the door close behind her as she left, and the old woman's fear seemed to touch his bones.


Definitely pee, he thought, and damp combined with a sickly perfume like those dying flowers Mr. Wheeler made the class draw in Art.

'I'll not hurt you,' he said, to the tiny figure propped up in a single bed below a narrow, heavily-barred window. He thought of his own little bedroom. His one refuge... 'It's my school', he explained. 'They've got this Social Awareness Programme to send us round hospitals and old folks' homes, you know, to stop us mitchin'...'

'Stephen,' she hissed through just a few teeth. 'I do like that name.' She stretched out her left hand, letting her small, white and ringless fingers dangle expectantly near the cuff of his duffel coat. But it was too soon. The same with girls. He'd never got it right. 'Hold them,' she urged him. 'Go on. No-one ever touches me. Only to push me this way and that... '

Beryl Purselove began to rock back and fore and, for the first time, in the marginally better light, he saw her face.

Jesus wept.

He'd only seen a skull once. Another of Mr. Wheeler's strange objects, with 'L luvs D,' in felt tip on the top and a cigarette butt stuck between its jaws. This was worse. There was hardly any hair, and her eyes were two sockets of skin crudely stitched together like those of some rag doll. His courage failed him. His rushed breakfast began to move upwards from his stomach.

'I must've got the wrong room. Sorry.' He backed towards the door and pulled, but this fire door was far too heavy.

'Please stay,' she pleaded. 'I've no-one else.'

He hesitated, envisaging Miss Duffy looking fed up again, when more than anything he wanted to please her.

'OK.' He searched the damp-patched walls for another light switch.

'You won't find no more in here.' Beryl Purselove said, following his every sound with her cocked head. 'They like it almost dark so they can't see when things need changing.'

Stephen sniffed again and gave up looking. That seemed true enough.

'Have you any family left?' he asked, remembering her husband was dead.

'All gone. I'm the last.'

'I'm sorry.'

Her hand again groped for his. This time he took it. 'Hey, you're freezing'.'

'Cold's cheap, see. And this winter's going on forever.'

Her visitor lifted up the thin eiderdown and felt her equally bony, icy toes. He shivered.

'This ain't fair. You're old.'

'Can't say nothing though. Only makes them worse. You get no supper otherwise...'

A congealed gravy dinner lay on her bedside table and he wondered how long it had been there.

'Well, I'll speak out and tell Miss Duffy.'

Suddenly Mrs. Purselove raised herself and leant towards him.

'You'll do nothing of the sort, young man. Or I'll be down in the cellar.'

'You what?'

He'd seen dungeons and stuff belonging to the Middle Ages in his history worksheets. But not now, surely?

'Mrs. Batten in room fifty-one once said no-one ever comes up from there, and,' she leaned closer, 'They steal everything, too. I'll never see my rings again, that's for sure. And I know this might sound fanciful, but it wouldn't surprise me if they could hear us now.'

Stephen's eyes widened.

'They?'

A tiny nod.

'Powers that be.'

'You mean we're being bugged?' He'd watched The X Files and Enemy of the State, but this was Birchfield House Nursing Home...

'I'm not as daft as some think.'

No, just crazy. Maybe that's what being in here does...

Nevertheless, he screwed up his eyes to imagine darkness forever. Then wished his mate Joe had come with him.

'I could smuggle one of our heaters in,' he volunteered. A small convector from when they'd had a garage. When he'd had a Mum...

The old lady fell back against her pillow.

'You be careful, son.'

Son?

Stephen covered her hands with the eiderdown edge.

'I'll bring you a thermos of tea as well.' He backed away. 'Just stay there now. OK? I'll sort it.'


The corridor seemed even blacker, that lobby even further away. This time, his ears tuned into snores, sad murmurings and the taint of dead things eking from other locked rooms as if all the old folk in the world were somehow crammed into that one ivy-covered house. And under it...

'The room key please.' A different nurse carrying a tray and a syringe, kept her hooded eyes on him as he dug in his duffel coat pocket. 'You'd no business taking it.'

'I'm comin' back, though. Mrs. Purselove needs a few things.'

'Excuse me?'

'She's freezin' and would like a cup of tea.'

The rock-faced woman tried to snatch it from him, but Stephen ducked past her and charged outside into Northampton's ever-busy Wellingborough Road.

He glimpsed the still-unopened daffodils in Abington Park's Field of Hope. A bus stickered with an advert for Silverstone motor racing, and he felt the air as cold as glass as he ran to the next stop, where an old man clutching a Tesco Millennium bag stared at him, crying.

No-one was following.

'Can't we 'ave her 'ere, Dad?' Stephen asked once he'd arrived back at the flat which had been home since Mum died. 'Kayleigh's room's empty.' His older sister was sharing a bedsit in Lings with her out-of-work boyfriend.

'You barkin' mad, boy?' Frank Ball was at his account book again, pencil gnawed to a stub. 'We ain't got enough for ourselves.'

'You should see 'er, though.' Stephen saw the smudged sums not adding up. 'She's all on 'er own and really poorly.'

His Dad looked up, Bits of a Pot Noodle round his mouth.

'Get a job then.'

'I can't. Miss Duffy's entered me for GCSE re-sits.'

'Hmm..'

'I could do weekends. Shoe World need people.'

'At one quid an hour?'

'Two, it is, and double time Sundays. That'd be twenty-four quid.'

Frank Ball's pencil stalled. He whistled.

'So why ain't you doin' it?'

'Dunno,' Stephen shrugged. 'But if she came here, I'd 'like, have a reason.'

His Dad stood up. Laboured towards the shaving mirror over the sink.

'She can't see me in this state. I'd have to friggin' shave every day and change me clothes.'

Silence as Stephen worked out the best way to break the news.

'It won't matter, Dad. She's blind.'

His father ran the tap too fast and slurped water from it. 'No way. What you thinkin' of? We're three floors up for a start.' He wiped his wet mouth on his sleeve and hobbled back to the table. 'Sorry mate.'

But Stephen wasn't listening. He had a plan. He'd go back to Birchfield House with Joe. Get the old girl out and have a taxi waiting. If he just turned up with her, what could his Dad do?

'Where ye goin'?'

'School,' he lied. 'Homework Hour.'

'Fish 'n' chips on the way back, eh?' His Dad winked.

'No probs.' But there were. The few pounds earned by cleaning teachers' cars was for the cab fare. 'Got no dough,' he added.

His Dad counted out two pounds eighty pence. The exact amount, then Stephen squeezed past the bike he'd not taken to school since its lights had been nicked, ran into the neighbouring Almond Court and up the stairs to bang on Joe's door.


'This it then?' His mate cast a streetwise eye over the large, stone-built house in one fell swoop. The rampant ivy and weed-filled chimneys. Flaking drainpipes and rusted window locks. 'Weird, man.'

'Wait till you get inside.' Stephen, too fixed on his mission to register how things had changed, rubbed a brown smear off his parka and re-tied his Nikes. 'Speak as posh as you can. OK?'

'Hell, I gotta practise.'

'Just follow me and act normal. Right. Move.'

They tried the Nursing Home's outer door, but it was locked and the stolen key too large.

'Funny, that. Last time, you could just walk in.' Stephen stood back, only then realising how thick and smothering the ivy had become. How all moth-holed curtains were drawn, the window sills blackened by grime. But where had all those iron bars gone? He frowned. 'Press the bell.'

No answer, just starlings pecking in the gutters heaped with rotted leaves.

Stephen heard a car draw up behind them. He turned to see a red Mondeo with the sign ALPHA CABS pull into the kerb; its driver leaning out of the window to speak to them.

'This it?' He asked.

'Yeah.'

'That's odd. My SatNav didn't recognise the name Birchfield House Nursing Home.'

Stephen hesitated. His mind spinning.

'Ready then?' The driver keen to get away.

'Sorry. Change of plan.' Stephen stared at the building, properly this time, Something definitely wasn't right. His heart seemed to beat faster as he heard the taxi revving up and leaving. He also felt much warmer as if summer had instantly arrived.

Both boys watched the taxi rejoin the main road's flow of traffic until it disappeared. Then Stephen removed his duffel coat and stuffed it under one arm.

'You sure it weren't somewhere else?' Joe unpeeled a chewed ball of gum from its wrapper and pushed it into his mouth.

'It was here. I swear it. Birchfield House Nursing Home, with a big sign over there... ' Stephen pointed at the overgrown front garden where neither any posts nor holes were to be seen.

How bloody odd...

'I'm well starvin'.' Joe suddenly lowered his anorak's hood and unzipped it.. 'Burger King's just down there.' He looked longingly towards a line of shops. 'You comin'?'

'Dad wants fish and chips.'

'He would.'

'Hang on.' Stephen was already by the ivy-smothered side gate. 'See if I can leg it over this. Maybe there's a way in round the back.'

But he was soon stopped in his tracks by a shrill female voice calling out from behind the adjoining fence..

'Oi! You pests! Clear off!'

Neither boy saw anyone until spotting the top of the neighbour's head. Her curly, brown hair held in place by two yellow hair grips.

'Just looking for an old, blind lady who lives here, that's all.'

The neighbour's grip tightened on the fence. Stephen noticed how the third finger of her small, tanned left hand bore a silver, diamond-encrusted engagement ring above a thicker gold band. She must have found a stone to stand on because her sharply blue eyes met his.

He felt suddenly sick.

'What's her name?' She demanded.

'Beryl,' was just a whisper.

A pause.

'Beryl? You sure?'

'Beryl Purselove. Mrs.'

Suddenly those hands fell away as a half-familiar cry left her lips.

'What's up?' called Joe.

'That's my name, you cheeky monkeys. And that house next door's been empty for years.'

'So, what's this then?'

He held up the key to room fifty-three.

'God knows. Just bugger off.'

With high heels clacking, she hurried towards her own back door before slamming it shut, but not before Stephen had glimpsed a red sundress. A neat waist and bare, brown arms. Just then those greedy starlings bolted into the blue sky, leaving a lull that only comes with death still waiting.

Stephen threw the key into her back yard and grabbed Joe's arm.

'This is fuckin' unreal and I'm boilin'. C'mon!'

They ran from sunshine into leafy shade, lungs bursting, and as Beryl Purselove with shaking hands put her new potatoes on to boil for her husband's lunch, the shriek of brakes and squealing tyres filled her kitchen. She rushed outside to hear two ominous thuds. Saw two warm, young bloods merged on the Tarmac. A removals truck skewed nearby, blocking the slowing traffic.

Then silence...

# We Went To Barry Island
## By Phil Carradice

We went to Barry Island
where the chip bags blow like rain
along the sand-strewn gutter
and the Gift Shops mark like Cain.

We went to Barry Island
for a day of long-lost dreams,
for candy floss and funfairs
and remembered childhood screams.

We went to Barry island
and at noon the rain came down,
it cloaked the empty beaches
and the nearby dying town.

We went to Barry Island
when the sea and sky were black,
when the trippers all departed
and the coaches all turned back.

We went to Barry Island
and we sat there in the rain,
holding hands in the shelter
and I was young again.

# Granddad And Me On My Tenth Birthday
## By Phil Carradice

When I was your age, boy,
says Granddad, putting down his pipe,
birthdays - well, birthdays meant delight.
Parties, presents, fussing,
your birthdays brought it all.

Tell me, I say,
about the presents.

Granddad smiles, the skin
around his eyes begins to crinkle
like a walnut.
Presents that would make you
weep for joy, he says.
Catapults and roller skates,
Dinky toys and circling clockwork trains.
Books of birds and great volcanoes
that spewed out lava,
white as soapsuds
across the page.

And sweets - oh, licorace and toffee,
fudge and mints
to make your mouth saliva

like a running tap.

Granddad stops and pulls
his hanky out to blow his nose.
His eyes are strangely sad and wet.
Birthdays now, he shrugs, are useful.
I stare, not understanding.

Useful, boy, he says.
Socks and underpants, that's what you get
when you grow old.
Socks and bloody underpants.

Except - he smiles again -
up here - he taps his head -
up here it's always catapults and roller skates.
And always bloody will be.

# Jack
By Phil Carradice

All morning cars have aquaplaned
around the corner,
sighing past my garden;
bright spray, in arches,
hosing like the wake of speedboats.

Here old branches hang
across the path,
heavy with the rains of August.

There is a fullness to the season -
full ditches bordering the fields,
full hedgerows, skies chock full of rain.

I, too, am full, with love and pride,
emotions bright, unfurled,
full with knowing he is in the world.

# Dusty As A Grandfather

By Phil Carradice

'Play, Granddad, play.'
He sits, reluctantly,
slides his aching body
to the floor. Three hours
of castles, dragons, knights
have drained him.

So many years he'd run
for eighty solid minutes
around the field, zephyred
like the swifts of summer.
And now he's drained
by one insistent three year old.
'Play Granddad, play.'

His young companion
waits beside him, tiny fingers
plucking at the strands of grey,
those silver whispers in his hair.
'Dusty as a grandfather'
the young man says,
not comprehending
the power of his image.
'Play Granddad, play!'

# Gale Warning
## By Jacquie Hyde

Beads of perspiration rolled from Abigail's forehead as her relentless nightmare hunted its prey. It silently pushed open the bedroom door. She heard its rasping breath as it slithered across the carpet. It crept towards her bed desecrating the room with every step. A foul odour smothered her as it stealthily slipped closer... closer. Abbie's skin crawled. Her breathing stopped. There was no escape.

A mature copper beech standing in the garden of number twelve Beech Grove cast fragmented shadows through the window. They danced a morning steel grey pirouette across the bedroom walls. Her burdened boughs swayed, laden with images and memories of a past time. She towered above the house and road. Frost crusted leaves shivered in the bitter breeze. Tap, tap - twiggy fingers played on the double-glazed pane.

Tap, tap...Abigail rolled over, wiped her brow with trembling fingers and buried her head into the pillow. The floral bedding tumbled onto the carpet. She crawled out of bed, grabbed the duvet, ripped open the poppers and rammed the cover and sheet into a wicker wash basket on the landing. The bedroom door opposite slipped open.

'Good morning sweetie. Sleep well?' A tall lean man with blonde hair falling across his face leaned over and pecked Abigail on her head. He wore a towel casually tied around his waist. His chest hairs brushed against her face. Abigail froze. His pale blue eyes penetrated her. She clutched her cotton nightdress tightly around her neck and backed into her bedroom.

'Abbie! Breakfast's ready!' A voice drifted up the stairs.

'Come on Abbie. Your mother's calling. Chop, chop. You don't want to be late. You know how I hate stress. Stress causes tension.' He slowly rotated his head. 'And that tension will need relieving.' He smiled and ran his tongue round his thin lips.

Heart pounding Abbie slammed the bedroom door. She dragged the shell pink dressing table chair across the room and rammed the back of it under the door handle but the carpet was fluffy and the underlay soft. The chair rolled over. She kicked it, slipped out of her nightdress and headed for the shower.

'Abbie! Can you hear me?' Her mother called.

Abbie rotated the shower controls, six, seven, eight, full on, but she could still hear the clamorous din of everyday life. The whistling kettle, the blathering radio and the smoke alarm as it shrieked it's warning, heralding the arrival of more toast.

'Bloody thing!' Abbie heard her mother cursing and pictured her wafting a tea-towel backwards and forwards across the alarm to shut it up. She heard the clump, clump of her mother's heeled burgundy fluffy slippers on the stairs and the chair slide across the carpet as her mother entered the bedroom.

'Abigail! Open the door!' Abbie cringed as her mother turned the door handle of the en-suite. 'You're going to be late for school.'

'Leave me alone.'

The door handle rattled, followed by a thud. 'Open the door. You know I hate locked doors.'

'I'm in the shower,' yelled Abbie. 'Give me some space.'

'You had a shower last night.'

'There's no privacy in this house. I want a lock on my bedroom door!' Abbie squeezed shower jel onto the facecloth and scrubbed her arms, her body, and her legs.

'I don't like locks on the doors. It could be dangerous.'

'What?'

'We could have a fire and you might get trapped.'

'I am trapped,' Abbie muttered under her breath.

'What did you say?'

Abbie gritted her teeth, tears swelled behind misted eyes.

'We don't need locks. We're supposed to be a family,' shouted her mother.

Abbie twisted the facecloth in her hands, tighter, tighter. She scrubbed her skin, harder, harder. Her red flesh burned.

'Breakfast's on the table. You're going to be late.'

Abbie slumped down onto the shower tray. Hot water splayed onto her back. She turned her face upwards towards the power jet. It pummelled her forehead and cheeks. The water ran down her neck and in-between her breasts. She breathed in deeply, dropped her shoulders and closed her eyes as she heard her mother leave the room. The hot steam encompassed her as the force of the water massaged her body.

'Shut up!'

'What?' Abbie wandered into the honey pine fitted kitchen, her clothes dishevelled. Strands of long blond hair dripped down her back onto her freshly laundered white blouse. She sat down at the rustic pine kitchen table, picked up a spoon and slowly stirred her cereal. She looked up from her cereal straight into her mother's green eyes.

'Mam. Can I have toast? I don't fancy cereal this morning.'

'That's what I was talking to.'

'Who?'

'That bloody thing,' Abbie's mother pointed towards the ceiling.

'You're not on about fires again are you? Just because I want a lock on my bedroom door.'

'No. The toaster keeps setting it off. It's too sensitive. It's driving me mad. I'm going to take the batteries out.'

'What's the point of having an alarm if you take the batteries out?' Abbie scraped the spoon across the base of her cereal bowl. 'Maybe you're right,' she muttered into the wheat flakes. 'Maybe it is too sensitive. Too sensitive for this house anyway.'

'What do you mean?'

Abbie starred at the pine laminate flooring.

'There's no time for toast. It's half past eight.'

'The bell doesn't go until quarter past. This cereal's disgusting.'

'And whose fault's that?'

Abbie jumped up, grabbed her bowl and scraped the cereal into the bin. On the work surface there was a toast rack with a selection of brown and white toast. 'You've done toast. Can I have some?'

'That's Gary's. Gary likes his toast chilled before the butter goes on it. He doesn't like the butter melted. Says it makes the toast soggy.'

'Yeah. Like soggy cereal. Forget breakfast!'

Abbie stormed out the kitchen and pounded upstairs. She fumbled for her hair dryer under a pile of clothes, grabbed the upturned chair and sat at the dressing table. The warm air fanned through her damp hair as she teased the brush through it. A photograph smiled back at her. Abbie dressed in the blue and green colours of the Sheraton Harriers with a medal draped around her neck. Her right hand was held high brandishing a shiny cup. Next to her stood a man with his arm wrapped around her. He had the same bright blue eyes and lop sided grin, even a dimple on his chin. She traced her finger over the picture, brought it to her lips and gently kissed it. Closing her eyes she willed the images of that day into her head, the excitement of it, elated at winning the Cross Country Championship, how proud her father was. She wanted to run for her country like her dad, but her mind clouded as the nightmare images returned. Goosebumps invaded her arms, she almost felt the rasping breath on her neck. She shivered.

Abbie dropped the hair dryer. Maybe...maybe it was all her fault?

Tap, tap...Tap, tap...She heard the copper beech against her window. Tap, tap... The sound didn't irritate her. It was comforting. It had always been there. She sat up and looked out of the window into the huge boughs of the tree. They reached up and up, stretched up and out towards her. She recalled long hot sunny days. The scorching sun, her brow sticky with sweat, her blistered hands as she worked creating the tree house with her dad. He was a master craftsman and lovingly passed his skills and passion of wood onto his daughter. He bought her a tool kit, precision engineered chisels capable of cutting the thinnest sliver and a selection of razor-edged handsaws that sliced through timber as if it were bread. They had worked meticulously, taking heed not to mutilate any of the beech's limbs. They had followed the contours of the tree, carved supporting beams around the boughs, weaved the timbers until they nestled as a womb into the very being of the beech. It was Abigail's den. Cocooned within the warmth of the wood and the sweet smell of sap.

Tap, tap…tap, tap…

Clouds raced across the pale winter sky. The beech groaned as she swayed in the blustering gusts. Fragments of pink and lemon sunlight skipped around the bedroom walls.

Tap, tap…tap, tap…

Abbie packed her school bag and training kit. Her empty stomach rumbled as she marched down stairs. Gary's voice drifted towards her. She shuddered - came to an abrupt halt in the hall. The kitchen door was ajar. Abbie saw her mother and Gary embracing each other. Gary's hand caressed her mother's bottom, the other pulled at her silk dressing gown to reveal her bare shoulder. Abbie's pulse raced, her bag slipped from her shoulder.

Gary's lips kissed her mother's neck. He opened his mouth wide and licked the lobes of her ears. 'Feeling a bit fraught my love?' Abbie's stomach knotted. She hung onto the bannister for support.

'Oh Gary, it's that daughter of mine.'

'She's young and wilful. Her hormones are all over the place.'

'You're so understanding. We don't deserve you.' A surge of heat flushed over Abbie. She felt dizzy, brought her hand to her mouth and swallowed a mouthful of bile.

'Shhhhhh,' Gary turned Abbie's mother around and kissed her on the lips. Abbie saw his snake hands slip under her mother's dressing gown. 'You're beautiful Josephine. Absolutely divine.' Abbie watched her mother melt into his arms.

'It's you that makes me feel like that. You make me feel like... like I'm special. I want to..'

BEEP. BEEP. BEEP.

'That damn smoke alarm!' Josephine slipped from his embrace, grabbed the tea towel and wafted it in a frenzy below the alarm.

'Later my love.' Gary pouted his lips, blew a kiss towards Abbie's mother, adjusted his tie and sat at the table.

More toast popped up, the kettle boiled. Abbie swallowed the sick from the back of her throat, took a deep breath and walked into the kitchen. Gary looked over the top of his paper and grinned.

'There you are sweetie. Your toast's ready. Just how you like it. You and me both.' Abbie stomped across the kitchen, opened the fridge and rammed a lunch box and plastic bottle into her bag.

'Abigail don't be rude. Gary's talking to you.' Abbie's mother gathered her dressing gown together. Abbie shrugged her shoulders. 'Huh... that's a joke. I'm not the one who's rude.'

'What do you mean?' Josephine ran her pink painted nails through her henna hair. 'I don't believe you sometimes.'

'I'm going!' Abbie brushed past her mother almost knocking her off balance, 'I don't want any breakfast.'

'Abigail. Stop.' Josephine splayed her arms open wide. 'What's going on?'

'Hey…sit down.' Gary patted the empty chair next to him. 'I'll pour you a cuppa. Have some toast. Marmalade?' Abbie shook her head, sipped the tea, chewed the toast. It was like sandpaper in her dry mouth.

'Don't bother Gary.' Josephine loaded the dishwasher. 'She's just in a bad mood.'

'Never mind love,' Gary leant over, ruffled Abbie's hair. 'I'll cheer you up tonight. Eh? Give you a treat.'

Abbie baulked at his touch.

'Let's go.' Gary tapped his watch. 'Time's getting on.' He grabbed his suit jacket from the back of the chair.

'I don't want a lift.'

'Course you do. You should be grateful. Gary has to go out of his way.'

'I want to walk with Emma.'

'Emma left ten minutes ago. Haven't you got training tonight?'

Abbie shrugged.

'At six. It's the trials for the cross country on Sunday. Kevin said you'd get in the team.'

'I don't wanna go.'

'What?' Josephine slammed the dishwasher shut. 'I knew you'd loose interest. I used to tell your Dad. It's no good pushing her. But he insisted. Said it was in your blood. I'll ring Kevin. Tell him you don't want to run anymore.'

Abbie reached down for her bag, her eyes stinging.

'Don't you dare,' she snarled as she twisted towards the door. Josephine grabbed the door handle, blocking Abbie's escape.

'I've got to let him know how you feel.'

'You don't know how I feel Mam. You never do,' Abbie spat. 'I do want to run. But...but you're on nights again an' you can't take me.'

'I'll take you sweetie. No problem. Come on now. School.' Gary slipped his arm around Abbie's shoulders. She shrank away.

'See yer.' She gave her mother a quick peck on the cheek.

'Good luck tonight. If you get in the team we'll come and watch on Sunday.' Josephine brushed a strand of hair away from Abbie's face. 'Your dad would have been proud of you.'

Abbie nodded, she slipped her feet into her shoes and heard her mother sucking up to Gary.

'Thank you for being so understanding.'

'Don't you worry.' Gary purred back. 'I'll look after her. You go back to bed. I'll pick you up in the morning. I don't want you walking home by yourself in the dark. I love...'

Abbie slammed the door on them. The bitter north-east wind greeted her on the doorstep. She took a deep breath, zipped her coat and leaned against the trunk of the copper beech. She stared up into the labyrinth of branches. Up and up. She heard the rustling of leaves, the creaking of the boughs, the persistent tap, tapping of twiggy fingers. She rested her cheek against the smooth bark. 'I wish I were Jack and you were my beanstalk,' she whispered. The wind battered into her, it whipped at her hair and sent her bag rolling across the lawn. 'You could take me...I wish...' She closed her eyes as she traced the letters carved out of the silvery bark with her fingertips. Richard Daniels - Abigail Daniels – 1978. The emptiness caught her breath. She looked up towards their den cradled in the swaying branches.

'We'll have to do something about that tree.' Gary bent over his shiny red car and carefully removed some of the leaves and twigs that were littered on the bonnet.

'What do you mean, do something about it?'Abbie glared at him.

'Look at the size of it.' Gary looked up into the boughs of the beech swaying above his head. 'It's dangerous. I'll get in touch with the council. Tell them to have it down? Come on sweetie. In the front seat. Travel in style next to me.'

'If you touch that tree I'll, I'll…' The words stuck in Abbie's throat. 'You've, you've got no right!'

'Rights? What rights are you talking about?' Gary sneered. 'It's about time you learned to do as you're told.' Gary fumbled with the fob. He pointed it at the car and he pointed it at Abbie. 'Get in the car. Now!' Abbie retrieved her bag from the garden hedge. She kicked out at the wheel of the car and stomped towards the back door. She would not sit in the front next to him. She pulled on the handle but the door was locked.

'Oh no! The remote's not working. Bloody batteries. Be an angel and get the spare keys from your mother.' Abbie flung her bag onto her shoulder and ran into the stillness of the house. The front door slammed shut, cutting off Gary's voice. The gale howled through the flapping letter-box.

'Mam! Have you got the spare keys? Maaam.' She ran upstairs to her bedroom. Her mother was making the bed. 'Gary needs the spare fob. He can't unlock his car.'

'I'll get it.' She bustled out the door. 'What a morning. You're going to be late.'

Tap, tap.. Tap, tap… Abbie sat at her dressing table. She carefully prised opened the carved jewellery box that her Dad had made her for her twelfth birthday. Her fingers played with the tiny circular battery before slipping it into the burgundy velvet pocket, next to her black jet earrings and the silver cross she was given at her christening.

Crack! Beep…Beep…Beep…

Abbie jumped, as a branch scrapped past the window-pane. She stared into a jumble of splintered timbers and twisted metal. The gale whipped at the carnage below, branches swayed and a motionless hand protruded from under the fallen bough. Beep…beep… mocked the car alarm.

Abbie's eyes travelled towards her den nestled into the limbs of the beech only feet away from the severed bough. Abbie's mouth twitched. She smiled as her foot gently nudged her tool kit under the bed.

Tap, tap…Tap…tap…The wind brushed twiggy fingers against the double-glazed pane…the leaves fluttered as fragmented sunlight skipped across the bedroom walls. Tap, tap…Tap, tap…

# The Photo Booth
## By Kate Glanville

It lay face down on the attic floorboards; a narrow strip of white, the dusty trace of a boot print along one edge. Carys put a hand on one of the roof joists to steady herself, and bent to pick it up. Time and damp had adhered it to the wood. She peeled it carefully away. It left a mark, a faint memory on the floor.

Carys turned it over and in an instant she was there. She could hear the swish of the curtain as they pulled it across, feel the cold plastic of the swivel seat through her home-made ra-ra skirt, the discomfort as she slipped sideways to make room for her companion, the race of her heart as his thigh pressed against hers. She could smell his leather jacket, damp from the Llandudno rain.

'Have you found the box yet?'

The shout came from the bottom of the ladder.

'I'm looking,' Carys called back.

She sat down on a plastic crate of long abandoned Lego and stared at the photographs. Four in a line, little squares of frozen time.

'It has Christmas Lights written on the lid,' the voice from down below again.

'OK.'

In the first square they were smiling at the camera, faces squashed together, cheeks flushed by seafront wind, in the second they had both put out their tongues, in the third she was bent forward laughing, her bleached blonde perm falling over her eyes while he made a V sign behind her head. In the fourth, they were kissing, properly kissing, mouths open, eyes closed, his hands on her face. In the attic Carys had to look away.

'On the left hand side.'

'On the left,' Carys repeated.

'In front of that hideous painting of Conway Castle your parents gave us.'

Carys looked down at the boy's face; dark shining eyes that crinkled in a cheeky grin, olive skin, beautiful black curls, ringlets she had teased him. She remembered sliding her finger into one; a delicate coil, a slippery snake. He wasn't like the boys in Ponty.

Marco.

Carys whispered his name.

Marco, she said it again, rolling the 'r', emphasizing the 'o'. It had sounded so exotic, so foreign for a Welsh seaside town.

'Not the white box that says Outdoor Lights.'

'Not the white box.' Carys banged her foot on the floor so that it would sound like she was looking.

'That's the box with lights left over from Meg's wedding, though I don't know why we've kept them. I doubt we'll ever throw a big party again.'

Marco had wanted to design furniture; like Alvar Aalto he had said. She told him that her parents had a chair from Habitat and he had called her sweet and kissed the top of her head.

'I don't know why we're even bothering with a tree this year.'

Carys wasn't listening.

'What with Megan going to Owen's parents on The Gower and Robbie doing God knows what in Australia.'

Marco had told her he wanted to go to New York to train at an art college he'd read about in a Sunday supplement. Her heart had stopped, she couldn't breathe; New York was another planet. It had been six hours and seven minutes since he had called to her as she stomped furiously across the pebbly beach.

Cheer up, it might never happen.

He had jumped down off the wall onto the stones beside her, graceful as a puma, long-limbed and lithe. He'd raised an eyebrow,

Were you dreaming of a pool in Benidorm?

Mam and Dad said this was far enough.

Do you like chips?

'No point….' Beneath the loft hatch he started to speak but the sentence turned into a cough, the hacking, lung-wrenching cough that had been with him since his man-flu in November. 'No point having a bloody tree at all,' he finally said.

Come with me.

He'd said they could live in a loft, hangout in Greenwich Village; coffee shops and galleries. Carys had looked into eyes like pools of melted chocolate,

I have to do my 'O' levels.

'I don't suppose we'll be having a turkey.' The ladder rattled as he repositioned it. 'You know I'd be happy with a toasted sandwich.'

'I know.' He said it every year, even when they had fifteen sitting down to dinner.

Come and meet my father, Marco had said that as they waited for the pictures to slide out of the machine. Best ice cream this side of Valencia.

Three scoops in a waffle cone, raspberry sauce, like lava, flowing down onto her fingers. Marco had taken her hand and licked her fingers, very slowly, one by one. Carys had blushed and glanced across the café but Marco's father had disappeared into the back room; they had the whole ice-cream parlor to themselves.

'I don't want a present this year.'

'OK,' Carys knew she'd have to get him something. It was Christmas after all.

'And you always say you don't really need anything.'

Carys could still feel Marco's beautiful curls, slick with Welsh drizzle as he nuzzled her neck.

'The money will be better spent repairing the caravan roof.'

Carys studied the kiss. The kissing had been like the candy-floss at the Easter Fair - she couldn't get enough.

'Shall I come up and look myself?'

'No! You'll fall and break the other foot.'

'This bloody plaster cast is driving me mad.'

'If you hadn't tried to carry so many logs….' Her voice faded, she'd said it a hundred times already.

Will you write? Marco had whispered into her ear as her parents waited with the engine running.

Every day.

'I think we should get rid of the log burner anyway.'

Carys looked up.

'It's not as if we have much time for sitting in front of it these days.'

Carys loved to watch the flames, flickering and dancing, warming her face while the dim light from his shed came through the window beside her.

'Too much bother, the house is hot enough.'

Carys thought about the money in her secret bank account. After Christmas she would leave. She had made the same decision every Christmas for twenty years. She knew she wouldn't - but if she really wanted to she could.

'Come on Carys, I've got things I need to do.'

She sighed and stood up. The box of lights was just beside her, clearly identified by his neat writing; large tipped marker pen, capital letters.

She looked at the strip of photographs one more time and slid them into the pocket of her cardigan.

She had written ten times before she'd had a reply. His first postcard had made her drunk with joy.

'Hand in glove, we can go wherever we please, and everything depends upon how near you stand to me.'

It was years later that she realized it was a line from a Smiths song.

'Careful,' he said as she peered down through the hatch. 'We don't need two of us on crutches for Christmas.'

She wondered what would have happened if his father hadn't had a stroke, if he hadn't had to take over the family business - if she hadn't kept on writing.

He smiled then and suddenly she could see behind the glasses and the grey receding hair, and the lines.

'Have you found the lights?' he asked.

Carys touched the pocket of her cardigan. She smiled back at him.

'Yes, Marco, I have.'

# A Few Small Nips
## By Mary Thurgate

'What do you think of this?' Pippa angled her workbook towards Richard. 'It's only a first draft but I am pretty pleased with it.'

She did look pleased; smug even, he thought as he approached the sofa where she sat curled in the corner, neat and feline, her small feet tucked sideways, her sleek, black hair cut short at the nape. So perfect, so immaculate. He breathed in the scent of her perfume as he made himself get close enough to read her manuscript:

BETRAYAL

BY PIPPA ROTH

The knot in his stomach tightened. It was all there: dates …..places ….names…seemed like she had hardly bothered to change anything.

He forced himself to keep calm, to try to think clearly. 'Not your usual stuff is it?' He barely trusted his voice.

She looked up, smiling. He looked away.

There was a piercing whistle from the kitchenette. 'Kettle's boiling, do you want tea?'

'Earl Grey, darling, not your builder's muck.'

There she goes again, nip, nip, nip, he thought. Why can't she just leave me be?

On automatic pilot, he poured boiling water into the brown earthenware teapot, swilled it round, emptied it into the sink, spooned in the tea leaves, and tipped in the rest of the water – spilling some on his hand. He looked down at his hand in a puzzled way. As he opened the cupboard to take out cups his eyes were drawn to the knife left lying on the worktop. Jeez. She's so bleeding obvious. A place for everything and everything in its bleeding place, and now this, the knife left out.

His fingers closed round the handle. He lifted it, felt its weight; a chef's knife, comfortable in his hand, long, stainless, sharpened to a razor's edge, beautiful, balanced, a joy to use.

He stood, weighing the possibilities.

'Is the tea brewed, darling?'

Her voice came to him as though through a thick fog. With a jerk he put the knife into its proper place and carried the cups to the sofa, spilling a little tea onto the white tiled floor. His hands were shaking.

Pippa yawned and stretched herself, casting the manuscript aside. 'I'm having a bit of trouble with the ending, but I'm sure it will come to me soon enough.'

## Supergran, Spiders, and the Semitone Snake.
### By Joy Daniels

Everything began when we moved from a house in town to a cottage in the country. It was like a cottage out of a picture book with the reds and oranges, yellows and greens of a giant Virginia creeper covering the walls. I could hardly believe that we were going to live there. The nearest neighbour was just a few yards down the lane – 'Keepers Cottage' – where Dad said the Saddler family lived. 'Nice family,' he said. 'Two children.'

Our house was called 'Mill House' because it had been a flourmill. The garden was what Dad and I liked best. In town we had only had an allotment. I used to grow radish and had great fun growing marrows, and when they were small, scratching names and patterns on them and seeing the patterns grow as the marrows grew. Dad said we should have much more scope in this new garden.

At the new school I made friends with Rowan, the younger of the Sadler boys; we were in the same class, which was good – our parents could share the school run. I showed Rowan our garden; he liked the den we had started to make, using willow cuttings to grow into willow hedge walls. I really loved the garden, but I found fear inside the colourful house. It was full of spiders! Long legged, huge spiders, whose scuttling movements into dark corners made me afraid to turn out the light at night. I told Rowan about the spiders, he thought they were probably living in the Virginia creeper. I told him I was very afraid of them. I was afraid every time I went to bed. I was afraid to sleep in case one should fall on me.

'Tell you what, Daisy, you should meet Supergran,' said Rowan. 'She will know what to do about the spiders, she is very good at sorting out problems. Supergran is my Dad's mother, we gave her that name, and she is such brilliant fun. She always does the Friday run because I spend most weekends at 'Yew Tree'.'

I told Mum about it. She had met Roger's Nan who seemed like a very nice lady, she said, living at Yew Tree Farm, just about half a mile down the road from Mill House. Mum and Dad did their usual spider hunt in my bedroom before bedtime and I was very soon off to sleep, happy with my new school, the new house, and a really good new friend.

The next day at school, Miss Golding asked us to pick as many types of grass as we could find. I picked quite a lot of types. Miss Golding said I was a real country girl. The bell rang. It was home time, and it was Friday, and I was going to meet Supergran!

Outside the school gate was a little blue sports car, the kind my teenage cousin would like to drive, and in the driver's seat, a silver-haired lady with twinkling blue eyes, and a lovely smiling face. 'C'mon, kids jump in! You've newly moved to Mill House haven't you?'

'Yes. I'm Daisy Martin.'

'I'm Rowan's Nan, you can call me Nan. Rowan stays with me most weekends. So, Daisy, how do you like living at Mill House?'

'Much better than where we lived before.'

Then Rowan prompted, 'Except for one thing; all the spiders, Daisy is terrified of them.'

Supergran smiled sympathetically. 'That is a pity!'

I agreed. 'Dad lets them run on his arms, and nurses them in his hands, but I am terrified. They run so fast. I don't like to even think about them.'

Supergran said she had been just the same, until someone told her that every time she saw a spider, she should say a prayer, then hold her breath to a count of eight, then let the breath out very slowly, and tell the fear to go away. 'Just remember how small a spider is! They have more reason to be afraid of us. We might crush them under our feet.'

I'd already tried this; lots of people told me there was nothing to fear. It hadn't worked, but I didn't tell Supergran. As we went through the gates of 'Yew Tree', two sheepdogs, Shep and Moss, came bounding out to meet us. They washed my face with lovely doggy kisses, and made me laugh. Supergran said that they must really like me.

Rowan thought a barbecue tea might be fun, so we started collecting firewood. Supergran brought out some sausages, then we made dampers with a paste of flour and water, shaping the dough into ropes, twisting the ropes round the ends of long sticks, then cooking them in the flames.

In the house we sat on a huge settle and had hot chocolate, whilst Supergran told us about some baby chicks that were about to hatch – we might see them by morning. I told them both about my new piano teacher, who had taken over from my usual one who was ill. She was very frightening and made me play scales all lesson.

At bedtime my room had a skylight window and I could see the stars twinkle their 'goodnights'. That night I dropped off to sleep soundly, with none of the usual fear to keep me awake.

The morning came bright and sunny, and we decided, since we wanted to share Supergran, that Rowan and I could be cousins. Well, sort of. That seemed quite cosy. I liked it.

When Dad came to fetch me, my head was buzzing with all that I had been doing. Dad came to look at the baby chicks and he thought there'd be a good spot for us to have some hens in our own garden.

Muriel – my older sister – was learning to be a hairdresser. She did not like living in the country at all. She said I was a proper 'tom boy', and that I ought to grow up. I didn't mind. Dad said it was because she was a teenager and I was more of a country girl.

That night, after the usual spider checks, I drifted off to sleep thinking of fluffy little chicks. Then suddenly I was falling, falling down a mountainside. I was frightened, very frightened. Whatever could I do? A bit of the day came back to me and I remembered Supergrans's breathing trick.

I saw I was very small, as small as a ladybird, and in my bedroom. I slowly walked as far as the landing, which felt like walking all the way to school, looking for somewhere to hide so as not to get stepped on. I found a safe place to hide in Muriel's handbag. It was all very well being in her handbag, but now I could not find a foothold to climb out if I needed to.

The inside of her bag made me sneeze and her lipstick was heavy and was lying on me. I needed to roll it away. I spotted her comb, which I used as a ladder to get me into the small phone pocket, which was much more comfortable, particularly since Muriel was now rushing for the bus to take her to college.

Then all went quiet for a long time – until she took her sandwiches to the park. Now I was on a park bench, still in the handbag, trying to climb out, when Muriel picked up her bag, brushed me off and with a scream yelled, 'Lurgies, yuck!'

I was flung through the air, only to be picked up by a massive bird. It gripped me in its talons as it sped through the air. I screamed, and screamed, until suddenly – it let go.

Down, down, down, I fell – into a pile of leaves, which luckily broke my fall.

Struggling to reach the top of the pile I heard someone calling out. 'Come this way – or you will get yourself killed!'

I tumbled down the pile to the ground and saw the voice came from a field mouse. I followed the creature to shelter under the roots of a rhododendron bush, where he introduced himself as Monty. A field mouse! He seemed more like an elephant to me for I was indeed very small.

I'm afraid I started crying. 'Come on,' said Monty. 'Don't you worry. You will be safe with me. I know just what has happened to you.'

I knew he meant well and he was after all offering to help me, so I smiled and thanked him. 'That is my pleasure,' he said. 'By the way, you do have a name I suppose?'

'Yes my name is Daisy Martin.'

'What a pretty name. I have cousins who are house mice at Mill House, that is how I know that you had gone missing.'

'We have only just moved into Mill House, and I feel lost and very small and frightened,' I continued crying.

'Well now crying won't help,' said Monty. But I felt cold and hungry, and I wanted to be my proper size. I was feeling very sorry for myself when I heard some rather loud chirruping. I dried my eyes, and saw four ants, whose very sharp pointy beaks made me more than just a little bit scared of them. Then, each of them spoke in turn, high pitched, clipped, staccato voices, a few syllables at a time:

'We have heard your story.'

'And so we have brought you some little treats.'

'In an acorn cup, some greenfly milk...'

'...And some little globes of raspberry juice.'

The greenfly milk was very sweet, the raspberry was really delicious and soon I felt a lot better. I had a safe place to stay and Monty was so kind and helpful.

Very soon the word went round and all the 'wildwooders' were bringing me gifts:

Samantha, a snail, brought along a big old shell that her grandfather no longer needed.

A wren brought some thistledown which made a lovely bed to curl up in.

Everyone was so very kind; I should have been enjoying this adventure. It would have been good to have had Rowan with me; but as Monty said, it would not be practical – he might have stepped on me.

188

The creatures and I discussed plans to get me back to my home. Mole thought a tunnel might be good; Monty remembered the times when a tunnel might collapse. I did not think I would ever get back.

'Now,' said Monty. 'There is one who is wise enough, strong enough, and fast enough to keep us out of trouble, and that is my friend Wolfie. He is a spider!'

My heart stopped. And so did my breathing. 'Oh no please. Not a spider! I'm frightened of spiders!'

Monty looked at me sadly. 'But Daisy, it really is the best chance of getting you safely home. You really need to meet him; he is so kind and understanding. We will surely find him in the bark of Kala Nag, the most ancient of oak trees.'

Reluctantly, I followed Monty as he struggled through fallen branches and leaves till we reached an enormous old hollow oak. Sure enough he was there, inside the hollow, in the middle of a huge web.

He looked so frightening, and so much bigger than me. He clicked his front legs together. Despite being almost rigid with terror, I tried to be polite. I managed a sort of a smile, and said 'Good evening ... sir,' when Monty made the introductions.

Wolfie sounded a bit like a teacher. 'Good evening Miss Daisy. Now I understand you have a fear of my kind – as do many humans. I trust this experience will prove to you there is no reason to be afraid.'

I gulped. 'Wolfie – it is not so much the actual spiders, as the speed at which you travel.'

'Yes. I understand. But we are very small compared with humans, and to avoid being stepped on, we have to move very fast.'

The ground started to shake violently, and from down beneath it came deep rumbling sounds. Everything became unnaturally quiet. I huddled closer to Monty, almost afraid to breathe.

The silence was broken by Derek, the Appleyard Drake, calling desperately to his darling wife. Looking outside I could see them on a nearby pond. 'Daphne! Take the babies. Keep on the water as long as you can. I will look after the little ones that are slower, but you will have to go up to where the sheep are! The shepherd will know what to do to keep us all safe. Go now dear, fast as you can!'

Wolfie and Monty pulled me back in. They remembered something like this before; they called it 'a happening'. We stayed very quiet. Through the silence we could hear, approaching, the sound of something big dragging through the leaves on the forest floor.

Wolfie peeped out and immediately withdrew his head. 'Yes. It is a very large snake, and it is heading towards us! Snakes eat field mice!' He had lost his suave air and now started running round in circles, terrified.

'Has it got bright yellow stripes?' I asked,

'Yes!'

'Then I think it might be the Semitone Snake. He almost saved my life once! He will be a friend. I explained that when I had had to meet the new piano teacher I had been scared of her from the very beginning. Mum had left me at the bottom of the stone steps, so I had climbed up to the shiny black door. A lady had opened the door – dressed entirely in black, her black hair secured with a pair of heavy weight knitting pins and a bunch of keys dangling by a chain from her waist.

190

'You must be Daisy,' she said. 'Well, come in. I intend to start as we will go on. Say, 'Yes Miss Witcher'. Get up on the stool child, put your books up and play something, I have to attend to another matter elsewhere. I shall be listening. You must remember that. I shall be listening to every note.'

'So I played semitone scales. I kept that piano singing semitones in every rhythm over and over. Eventually Miss Witcher came in saying she wanted to be sure that I realised the importance of practice and so she was going to put me into her cellar to reflect on all she had told me. 'Pupils come to me to achieve a level of brilliance and that does not come easily!' And almost before I knew it, I was locked in her cellar, which was full of hissing snakes. I had to keep calm and think what I should do. The woman could not be normal. Then what I thought was a boa constrictor wrapped itself around me, and spoke: 'Don't fret my dear, nothing shall harm you, I have found a way for us all to escape. Miss Witcher is not as powerful as she likes to think, I am supposed to be a boa constrictor, but I have turned out to be only a very overgrown caterpillar of the cinnabar moth! Very soon I will become a chrysalis and become my proper size. You hang on tight. I am going to try and force open the coal delivery hatch, then we shall be free.'

'I did as he told, and soon we were out of there. Ever since, I called him the Semitone Snake.'

'That sounds a narrow escape,' said Monty. 'He was a real friend to you. He had better come here under Kala Nag with us.'

So I invited Semitone in and despite Wolfie's alarm, he proved to be quite friendly. From deep underground continued to come sounds of cracking and booming. Semitone snuggled around the three of us. We could hear the desperate calling of a duck bringing her brood of ducklings and Drake following her, telling her that they should make for the sheep pens.

A snapping of twigs and a crunching of crisp autumn leaves accompanied the rhythmic squeak, eek, eek of a large black pram being pushed along by a tall figure dressed entirely in black, a chain at her waist from which dangled a huge bunch of keys. The figure then picked up from inside the pram, a stick that she put over her shoulder and rubbed vigorously, until it burped, loudly. The stick, safely in its pram, was then subjected to a lullaby for quivering silver in a dodgy key. The ground started to rock gently and gradually becoming more aggressive, faster and faster. We stayed very quiet at the foot of Kala Nag.

Chanticleer was flapping and, calling in alarm to Pertelotte, the prettiest fowl you ever saw. It was too late for them now. 'Off with their heads!' screamed Lady Chuckie Gruber. Lord Charles James Fox shouted at the top of his voice 'Yahoo, Kill kill!' A booming tannoy system announced, 'Daisy! Daisy Martin!'

'Oh Monty whatever should I do?'

'Keep stum.'

'I can't, they know I'm here. I must answer.'

'Miss Martin I hope you are aware that you are responsible for all the murder and mayhem here today," came from the tannoy.

'That is not possible! I have done nothing wrong!' My knees were knocking. Again, I was very frightened.

'Of course you are guilty,' yelled the tannoy, ' you had cheese for supper, and everyone knows cheese for supper is asking for trouble.'

Semitone whispered into my ear. 'Close your eyes, say a prayer, take a deep breath, hold it as long as you can, let it go slowly and tell the fear, all the fear, to go away.'

I fell asleep, when I opened my eyes, I was my usual size and there was Wolfie, or maybe one of his relations, resting on my pillow.

I was so pleased to see him, I realised he had far more to fear than me, and I should look after him. I picked him up gently and placed him on the windowsill where he could be near me and be safe. I lay in bed watching him stretch and twitch his legs towards the colourful fronds of creeper trailing in through my open window.

I decided that this morning I would be really brave and tell my parents that I was going to give up piano lessons. The last of my dream slid away from me like a yellow and black striped scarf.

I felt sure that Semitone Snake and all my woodland friends would approve of my newfound determination.

### Crossing Swords
### By Julian Gray

Dafydd was enjoying a moment's peace and a glass of brandy, sitting on his favourite swivel chair at the desk in his study. He had just finished hosting a New Year's Day lunch with friends. Comparing himself with them, he was quite reassured of his status as a sturdy old man, happily married for over fifty years and apparently fairly indestructible apart from his arthritis.

Laughter and crockery-stacking noises were coming from the kitchen, as his wife and the rest of his family were finishing the washing up.

He swivelled. The view through the window across the local farms was bleak at this time of year and he looked for-ward to being able to get out and about more in a couple of months. He turned back and fiddled with a few papers before deciding that nothing needed doing.

He cupped the glass in his hand to warm it and enjoyed a sniff of the brandy. For entertainment he started rummaging through a drawer that for several years had been where he kept old photographs. The treasured memories used to be on display in earlier larger houses but were now demoted and out of sight in his desk. He came across several of the fencing teams he was in during his younger days; formal poses, smiling faces of team members in their white kit holding various swords, with proud coaches standing alongside. He felt warm about the friendships with his team colleagues. One picture was of three fencers standing behind a small trophy. It was taken in their last year at school. Dafydd had an épée; Alun – his best man later on – held a sabre, and Gwilym sported a foil. They had won a one-weapon-one-man championship in the county. Later on Gwilym had become an MP and was knighted when he left the House recently – Sir Gwilym. Alun became a surgeon and a professor of pediatrics.

The three of them had shared school and university to-gether, close friends for eight years. They had been involved in international competitions and, even in their late thirties, not practising any more, they were still formidable opponents. Dafydd patted his tummy, remembering how his old canvas fencing jacket had got tighter and tighter as the years went by.

In a photo taken during his last year at university he was in the middle seat because he had been the captain of the team. Gwilym and Alun were both sitting as well. He put the picture down and faced the window again but didn't see the view because he was enjoying one of his most vivid memories of that time: training with his colleagues, in the gym crowded with many fencers fighting each other enthusiastically, including most of the ladies team. He was interrupted by another fencer who informed him that someone at the door wanted to speak to the person in charge. Taking off his mask and panting, he walked over to meet a pretty woman with blue eyes and blonde hair in a bun, a fencing kitbag slung over her shoulder. She looked slightly nervous.

'Hello' he blurted out, smiling. 'How can I help? I'm Dafydd, captain of the team here.'

'Ah well,' she began, and instantly Dafydd was intrigued because of a foreign accent. 'I am an au pair with the Professor Morgan's family. I came to learn English better. The other day I told them I did fencing. They said I should go to the University's gymnasium – is that the right word? – and ask if I could join in with the Fencing Association. They said that probably only students would be allowed but I thought I would try any-way. So here I am.'

*Not only a foreign accent but a slightly husky voice. Wow.* 'We call it the Fencing Club. How long are you here for?'

'Only six more weeks, then I go home for Christmas. My family is in Budapest.'

'What's your name?'

'My friends call me Gerti - g - e - r - t - i.'

'Well Gerti, I'm sure that it will be OK for you to join in for a few weeks. We meet here every Monday, Wednesday and Friday afternoon and have matches on Saturdays and sometimes we go to Cardiff or London for Championships over the weekends. And we have a ladies team–' He pointed towards the far right corner '–and they would be very strong opponents for you but you might enjoy fencing them. I'm sure they would welcome you.'

'Thank you.' She relaxed and gave him a wide smile. Perfect white teeth. Dafydd's heart skipped a beat. 'Thank you, I am very pleased.'

'I see that you have your kit. Why don't you change downstairs and let's find out what you can do?'

Dafydd went back to his training, keeping half an eye on the door, and in ten minutes she was back. He saluted his practice opponent with a quick wave of the sword. Gerti had seen him and he beckoned her over. She looked wonderful and walked with the confidence of an athlete. *Tight fencing kit really does something for slender women.* He noticed that she had her glove on her left hand. Left handers are tricky.

'OK, let's have a go,' he said. 'I need to get my foil.'

They put on their masks, saluted, and squared up to each other. After a few feints by them both, what followed was the most glorious fencing experience that Dafydd had ever enjoyed. Gerti was nimble, strong, clever, cunning, tactically subtle and absolutely determined to hit him. What a competitor. Most important she was able to engage in quite complex cycles of thrust, parry and riposte, and not many people could do that. Magical. They battled quite aggressively for about twenty minutes and then Gerti stepped back, signalled that she was going to take off her mask, so they both did and saluted. She was panting hard and perspiring freely and some strands of her hair had strayed across her face, sticking to it. 'Utterly beautiful' thought Dafydd.

She took out a towel from her kitbag. Dafydd – panting hard too – joined her, and they slumped down side-by-side on a bench.

'You're really quite good,' Dafydd said 'I think that you'll give our ladies a hard time. You have obviously been very well trained.'

'Yes. I'm Hungarian Ladies Champion.'

Dafydd smiled at the memory, returned the photos to the drawer and leaned back enjoying a deep breath of the brandy fumes. 'Good stuff this - I must make it last' he thought and took a small sip. The phone rang.

'Hello, Dafydd Williams.'

'Hello Dafydd, it's Anne. I guess that you must have finished your lunch. We're sorry we couldn't be with you. Is Gerti there?'

## Ysgaddril

### By Will Macmillan Jones

I don't know about you, but I love trees. I spend as much time as I can walking in the woods and talking to the trees. They are alive you know, and everything that lives talks and communicates to its fellows in some way. Look at the oak trees. Did you know that you even get male and female varieties? So they love and mate as we do: only it all takes place over a much longer life cycle than ours, obviously. They talk, they must talk, and I try to hear them and understand their romance.

If you've any spark of romance in you, then like me you probably get drawn to the lone tree. Don't you love the image of the single tree on the skyline of a ridge? Especially when the rosy fingers of a summer dawn glow on the leaves, or the cold, sweet light of the moon shines stark through the bare branches as the autumn wind howls. At times like that the lonely tree still talks, but to whom?

Well, to me for one. Every year at this time there's one special tree on a skyline for me. It isn't far from where I pass the days, and one night in the year I go and sit there beneath the bare spreading branches and I talk to the tree of the season fled, the approaching winter and the spring beyond. Does it hear me? I'd like to think so, for I always rise from the grassy seat feeling I have been refreshed and gifted with enough energy to last me the coming year. One reason I think of it as my tree of life.

Sometimes as I walk away down the ridge with the grey dawn rising at my back, I look back and outlined with the branches I can see my body hanging from the tree, just as I left it there all those years ago.

# In Captivity
## By Sara Fox

The tarmac petered out and continued as a green lane, dark under its arching hedges. I pulled the car over onto the verge behind an old grey tractor. An elderly woman appeared, as if summoned, from a field gate in front of us, and I got out of the car to pacify and placate while Sally gathered up our picnic.

'Lovely day! Is it alright if we go this way?'

The woman stared at me for a moment. She wore a headscarf, a dirty raincoat and wellies. She clutched a large bottle with an appropriately sized teat. Here we go, I thought. But suddenly she smiled. 'Are you looking for the Cairns? Yes, they're up there.' She gestured vaguely towards the hollow way where sunlight flickered under the trees. 'Been feeding my baby I have.'

From the corner of my eye I was aware of Sally raising her eyebrows next to me. 'He's in there.' She indicated back the way she had come. 'I love my calf, I do. I give him two of these and then I know his tummy's full.' A gap-toothed grin. 'On holiday are you?'

I explained that we lived in the next valley over.

'Oh, Llanyrcefn. Lovely up there it is. I'm from Pontardunant I am. My mother was that worried about me being a farmer's wife, but I managed alright. I don't like the mart, though. I never go. My husband and my son take the animals, I don't like the people you get there sometimes.' She frowned at the thought and then brightened up. 'Is this your daughter?'

I said yes, and that she was back home from the city for a while. 'London is it? I was born there. My mam used to wrap me in a shawl and take me under the ground.' Seeing our puzzled faces, she added, 'In the war. My father had been a collier though and they were called to go back down the mines, so we came home to Wales.' She grimaced. 'No joke for those who had the dust in their lungs already. I haven't been back to London except for a weekend after we got married.' Then her face lit up, 'And to see Nanuk. I used to cut out pictures of him from the papers for my scrapbook.' She shook her head at our ignorance. 'You know, Nanuk, the polar bear, born at the zoo. I was ten, my mother took me, dad was ill all the time by then.' Her black eyes were shining with the memory of it. 'The keeper held him up in front of the crowd and we were allowed to stroke him. His fur was beautiful soft. He was crying and twisting about trying to get free.' Her face fell. 'He didn't live long. They don't in captivity.'

She was interrupted by a small bellow from the field, and we walked over to look at the furry calf. 'There now Blackie, no more *llath* for you until tea time.' Then more fiercely, 'My husband says I spoil them, but animals feel more than people think.' She looked at us for confirmation. Kindred spirits. Three women.

She stroked the hard head of the calf through the gate, 'I wasn't born to farming. My boss moved the insurance office here and my job was to take the farmers details. My husband came in one day and asked me where the dances were held. He didn't ask me to go with him, but he turned up one evening at the drill hall and that was that.'

She looked down at my sandals. Mud from the recent rain was percolating up between my toes. 'Do you have wellies? The river crosses the road down there.'

She returned to the theme of her life. 'My husband likes the old ways, but our son went to the Farm Institute. I feel sorry for him, he'd like to try something new on the farm sometimes.' She laughed. 'I keep the peace I do! But I like it here and I go to a nice chapel over the fields.'

This did not seem much compensation to us, but we smiled back at her.

She waved us on and we walked into the green gloom of the trackway that curved upwards onto the open hillside. As we ate our sandwiches and watched a family group of ravens catching the air currents below us in the valley of the Bran, Sally said, 'Do you think she ever goes anywhere or talks to anyone?' I shook my head, meaning I didn't know.

Some mad instinct made me want to call at the farmhouse to say goodbye to the woman on our way home. We crossed the yard strewn with obsolete pieces of agricultural machinery and knocked on the door. The place looked neglected under its thatch of green moss, as if no-one lived there. We heard voices at first and then a game show, loud on the television. It was a house that was closed to visitors. We did not linger.

\* *Llath* is the local pronunciation of llaeth (milk).

# About the Authors

## Helen Adam

Helen is a musician living in Llandovery. Her usual working life sees her out and about fiddling at weddings, parties, and festivals in Wales and beyond. This gives her lots of opportunities for people watching, especially at moments of high social and familial drama. Unashamedly curious, she enjoys creating back-stories and characters derived from glimpses into other people's lives. As well as performing, she also writes and arranges music, especially the tunes of her adopted homeland. Helen lives with writer David Thorpe, in an atmosphere of simmering mutual resentment and subconscious competition.

## Peter Barker

Peter's short piece, 'Someone To Hold' won the Flash 500 competition early in 2018. He has also produced a small history of the small Dorset village where he grew up and published a novel, 'System Error: invitation to revolution'.

He is a Greenpeace volunteer and with his wife, lives off-grid in mid Wales with 31 rabbits. As he says, 'For me, the best thing about writing fiction, is to sit down with an idea in your head and then to just let the story take over.'

www.viewfromabridge.yolasite.com

## Phil Carradice

Phil is a poet, novelist and historian. He has published over 50 books, the most recent being 'The Cuban Missile Crisis' and 'Bloody Mary' (both Pen and Sword). He presents the BBC Wales History programme 'The Past Master' and is a renowned creative writing tutor for both adults and children. Now a full time writer he was, for many years, a teacher and headteacher in schools for highly disturbed adolescents.

## Joy Daniels

Joy is a product of the South Wales Valleys, where humour, doubtless born of tragedy, is the best salve for any hurt, and faith holds everything together. She can honestly say that a kindly humour should be prized, but humour can be a two-edged sword that cuts deep; so the Valleys person can be someone to be reckoned with!

## Sara Fox

Sara is a freelance historian who specialises in houses, gardens and landscapes. Her background was in horticulture and more recently archaeology. She is currently writing a historical novel about the daughter of a Captain in the East India Company and an Indian 'Princess' which is set in Carmarthenshire in the early 19th century. She is also writing the history of a 500-year-old artefact and its many owners. She has been writing on and off, creatively as well as factually, about people and how they relate to their landscape since childhood.

## Kate Glanville

Kate was born in West Africa in 1968 to Irish parents. Kate spent her school days in Bristol and then studied fashion design at St Martin's College of Art in London. She moved to rural Wales in 1992 where she set up a pottery business in the village of Bethlehem. As well as painting pottery for customers all over the world, including Prince Charles and Madonna, Kate loves to write. Since 2012 she has had three novels published in the UK, Germany, Norway and the USA. A Perfect Home, Heartstones and Stargazing. Stargazing was long-listed for Welsh Book of The Year and A Perfect Home and Heartstones have both been in the top 100 women's fiction charts.
www.kateglanville.com

## Julian Gray

In 2006, after Julian Gray had completed 45 years in engineering and industrial management, ⬜⬜⬜⬜⬜⬜⬜⬜⬜⬜⬜⬜he and his wife Gwenda (who had been in Llangadog village school as a little girl) retired to the south west corner of France. They went to indulge their life-long passion for buying and restoring derelict houses. It was their fifth major project and it took several years to complete. One day while relaxing in the evening shade outdoors, Gwenda looked over the top of her wineglass and said "Being here is wonderful but I'd really really like us to spend the rest of our lives in Llangadog?" They found a very wonky, typical-Welsh, old stone farmhouse close to the village. It needed to be knocked down and has been redesigned and rebuilt as a perfect home.

## Jacquie Hyde

Jacquie is a northern bird with strong welsh connections on her mother's side of the family. She says, 'I've got more years under my belt than I care to remember. I guess I'm more of an old broiler than a chicken.

I live on a small farm with my hubby set in the most stunning scenery ever, with views of the Cambrians and the river Twyi coiled around us. I love writing when I get the time but life seems to have an annoying habit of getting in the way. I'm half way through writing a young adult novel that I dream one day will be finished and, dare I think it, even published. One thing I am good at is slowly, ever so slowly plodding on. So who knows? One day I may look up and see the spine of my novel on a bookshelf, tucked in between the proper authors.'

## Daisy Hufferdine

Daisy Joined the Group in October 2016. This is her first story in print. In another life she enjoys gardening and is a roadie for a blues duo.

## Steve Kill

Steve grew up in Lyndhurst in the New Forest National Park and soon developed an affinity with the countryside and the natural elements. Enjoying a long career as a property developer in Hampshire and Surrey, Steve and his wife Terri made the decision to move to the Brecon Beacons to enjoy a closer relationship with nature. Here they settled with their two spaniels, Penny and Mia, in sight of the stunning Black Mountains. Since retiring three years ago, Steve has finally found enough time to pursue his passion of writing poetry, drawing reference and inspiration from the beautiful surroundings he now lives within.

## Will Macmillan Jones

Will is a fifty something lover of blues, rock and jazz, who recently fulfilled a lifetime ambition by extending his bookcases until they filled an entire wall of his home office. He's also often found walking on a high hilltop or hidden valley, frequently lost with the aid of a Satellite Navigation Device, and hunting for dragons in dark caves... He says, 'He hasn't found one yet, but it's only a matter of time!' www.willmacmillanjones.com www.amazon.com/-/e/B005TIMXI0

## Ciaran O Connell

Born in Dublin, Ciaran lives in Cilmeri. Right now he is working on his second novel set in his home town during the tumultuous years leading up to the 1913 lock out. It involves a marriage across class and religion, money-lending and the battles between employers and unions. He will proudly tell you that his first novel has earned him nineteen rejection letters. That's about a murder on the playing fields of North Dublin in the fifties. He plans to re-visit it once he finishes this second one.

**Colin R Parsons**

Colin wrote his first book Wizards' Kingdom to help his youngest son with his reading, at primary school. He eventually made it into a magical series of three books. Since then he's written many novel's in various genres; Sci-Fi, Fantasy, Supernatural and Steampunk. Colin, eventually realised his dream and became a full-time author in 2013. His day-to-day job includes visiting lots of schools throughout the UK - running workshops and addressing, large audiences with presentations.

Colin loves to go walking with his wife, whenever they get the chance and he also enjoys reading. When he's not doing school visits, you can find him in the north tower of his castle, writing and contemplating world domination.

His books can be found at;

www.amazon.co.uk/Colin-R-Parsons/e/B0034Q4XS2

**Tom Phelps**

Tom is a Rhondda man who writes and performs poetry about valley life above and after the Pits. He has been married to Jean since 1960 and they have three grown-up children and nine grandchildren. Apart from his poetry, his main interest is music in general and Jazz in particular. He plays the piano and the saxophone, but not, he says, at the same time.

http://www.tomphelps.wales/

**Hazel Regdrave**

Hazel Redgrave née Miller was born at Maryport, Cumberland 1940. Originally from Liverpool, her family spent many years in East Africa where she worked for East African Railways & Harbours. On returning to the UK in 1960 Hazel joined the Women's Royal Air Force, and after demob joined the Civil Service working at both the Cabinet and Home Offices. She married Jim in 1978, moved to Wales in 1986 and is now retired. Hazel enjoys many handicrafts and in particular loves growing plants to raise funds for Llandovery Youth and Community Centre. Her other interests include collecting books, reading and listening to music.

## Maya Sales-Hyde

Maya is a 17 year old student who has spent the majority of her life reading about other people's adventures and writes as a way to create her own. One day she would like to publish a novel, but first she wants to travel the world, having her own adventures and meeting enough incredible people that she won't run out of plot ideas for a long time. If all else fails she intends to join an ABBA tribute band, and live out the rest of her days singing Waterloo in ill-fitting spandex.

## Sally Spedding

Sally was Born near Porthcawl, Wales and has a Dutch/German background. She trained in Sculpture, before winning an international short story competition when she was approached by an agent. Her crime thrillers begin with 'Wringland', set on the Fens, published in 2001. Her tenth and latest, 'Behold a Pale Horse,' set in Wales, London and the south of France, appeared in 2017. She is also an award-winning short story writer and poet, An active member of the CWA, Mystery People and Crime Cymru, Sally spends part of each year in the haunting eastern Pyrenees.
www.sallyspedding.com

## Stella Starnes

Stella is twenty seven years old and has Mosaic Down Syndrome; a very rare form of Down Syndrome which makes it a bit difficult for her to socialize at times. Stella lives in Llandovery on the High Street above a boutique called Cibola where she sell cards and prints, which are also sold in Myddfai, Carmarthen and Tenby and she often helps out as a shop assistant there too. She also loves drawing, and colouring in patterns and her favourite artists are Alan Lee, John Howe and the Pre-Raphaelites. She's always loved reading, especially fantasy stories like 'The Chronicles of Narnia', 'The Hobbit' and 'The Lord of the Rings' and plenty of Celtic fairy tales, which have always inspired her. Stella has constantly tried to write a complete story, all with different ideas and now, at long last 'Walking with a Dead Horse' is her very first fully completed story. Stella also loves swimming, travelling, shopping, walking the family dog and watching films like 'Harry Potter', 'Pokémon' and Sam Raimi's original 'Spider Man'.

## John Thompson
John was born in 1942, spent the years 1961 to 1975 mainly as a student, gathering three degrees (a first degree, a Masters in History, and a Law degree) and then the Bar qualification. As a barrister he heard many weird stories that were stranger than fiction, and began to write then, often drawing on his experiences of events and people. In 1991 he moved to Wales and joined the Carmarthen Writers Circle, later becoming chairman. He also joined the Llanelli Writers Circle, and has been chairman there for the past 3 years. In 2015 John published the first volume of The Brindavan Chronicle (Genesis), the second following in 2017 (Nemesis). The final volume is being written now. This year he published Judas: the Man Behind the Myth - an alternative (fictional) account of the life of Judas. John has also published a number of short story booklets. Currently he's working on two fantasy books for children.
www.thompson-authors.com

## David Thorpe
David convenes the Llandovery writers group. He is a full-time writer, (e.g., speculative novels 'Hybrids' and 'Stormteller', scripts, and non-fiction about environmental issues). A co-founder of the London Screenwriters Workshop, he's worked with/for Marvel Comics and many other publishers. He loves teaching, cycling, nature, and fending

off his wife, the ebullient note-smith Helen Adam. Despite this, he continues to believe that with imagination we can change the world. www.davidthorpe.info

## Mary Thurgate
Mary lives in the big blue house in Stone St. Llandovery. She started out as Jeanie Marie counting imaginary sheep, became Madeline rescuing the Bad Hat, spent much of her later childhood as Lucy in Narnia, Anne in Green Gables, Susan from the Moon of Gomerath. As a young woman she was of course Jane Eyre and Catherine Earnshaw running wild on the moor. Now Mary finds she is more than happy to be Mrs Bennett.

## Graham Watkins
Graham, a retired businessman who snatched up a pen when his commercial sword rusted away, lives in an old farmhouse on the Black Mountain. His first book Exit Strategy describing how he sold his company was followed by a series of books retelling Welsh legends, 'The Welsh Folly Book'- an excuse he says to explore Wales, 'The Iron Masters' an historical novel set in Merthyr Tydfil and 'A White Man's War' inspired by a holiday in South Africa. He's published more than twenty books with both traditional publishers and as a indie author. He claims he writes for pleasure because there's no money in writing.
www.grahamwatkins.info
http://author.to/GrahamWatkins

# Introduction to Llandovery Writers

## The Muse of Inspiration Has Touched Us!

I am astonished that there is such a plenitude and variety of talent in the area of Llandovery, a secret corner of Carmarthenshire, South Wales, packed with hidden treasures.

This collection of 33 stories and poems represents just the tip of the iceberg of the productivity of most of the writers represented within. Most of them have been attending my writing class – some for the last two years since it began. Many are working on novels, and one or two have been published so far. Other writers are friends and supporters of the group.

Short stories are harder to write than long novels, strange as it may seem. They require making every word count and often an unexpected twist at the end. We chose a flexible theme: 'the turnings of years', which could be interpreted in many ways. Some have done so with a seasonal flavour, others have concerned themselves with cyclical events.

The tales adopt many genres and styles; you'll find in the following pages: ghost stories, true stories, stories for children, historical stories, a comedy, a thriller, a metaphysical story, domestic stories. All are packed with emotion, crafted to make you weep, laugh and think; for a good story makes you see the world differently, notice things you did not before. It sticks in your mind long after you've finished it.

The Llandovery Writers Group has developed a strong bond of trust, so that its members feel empowered to both give and receive constructive criticism, confident that it will be well taken. They make a great team, so what you'll find within these pages is not just the product of individual minds, but has been honed by a process of mutual critique and support, which has helped each writer to develop and polish their story from first draft into its eventual form. They have all learned well and progressed enormously.

It is hard work, as all will attest. But we hope you'll think it is worth it.

We meet in the Llandovery Youth and Community Centre, by Market Square, on Wednesday evenings at 7pm. The centre hosts a wide variety of events and activities, especially for children and young people, and their families. It is a vibrant, community resource and I encourage you to use it. Without it Llandovery would be a much poorer place. It operates on a shoestring, however, and this is why we are using the proceeds from this book to raise funds for it – as well as to say 'thank you' for hosting us all this time.

Thanks also to Graham Watkins, who has put a lot of trouble into editing and publishing this collection, as well as chasing everyone up and a big thank you to all my students for their loyalty and brilliant work.

The theme of my structured course is 'Making readers care'; in other words how to pay attention to character creation, structure and style to the extent that the stories become 'unputdownable', so gripped is the reader by a sense of involvement generated by the words on the page. I even threw a couple of my own stories into this mix, and was pleased to get back as unflinching feedback as I have given out!

If you want to find out more about the writing course, call me on 07901 925671 or email hello@davidthorpe.info. You don't have to come to the class to take it – you can do so remotely, online. See:

http://davidthorpe.info/online-writing-course/.

May the muse be with you!

# Llandovery Youth and Community Centre

What goes on in the Tardis-coloured building with the flower-bedecked jeans outside? Probably more than most people imagine.

Borne out of a need for a social meeting place for teenagers in the town some 28 years ago, the Centre has, like Topsy, just grown and grown, and now caters for all age groups. There are facilities for using computers/internet every day, an after-school club, youth club and a range of self-help groups and organisations who use the Centre as a base for their work in the town.

It is possible to join a Writers' Group, study Latin and Ancient Greek, Knitter Natter to your heart's content, join a monthly Navy, Army and Air Force Institute, get together to do craftwork or paint, use the recording studio, hire a room for your group or just call in for a chat and a cuppa.

Advice groups attend the Centre and staff/volunteers are happy to help with any problems or signpost enquirers to other organisations.

Jill Tatman, Manager, LACC

Find us on Facebook at.
www.facebook.com/groups/LlandoveryyouthandCommunityCentre

#0132 - 081018 - C0 - 210/148/12 - PB - DID2322899